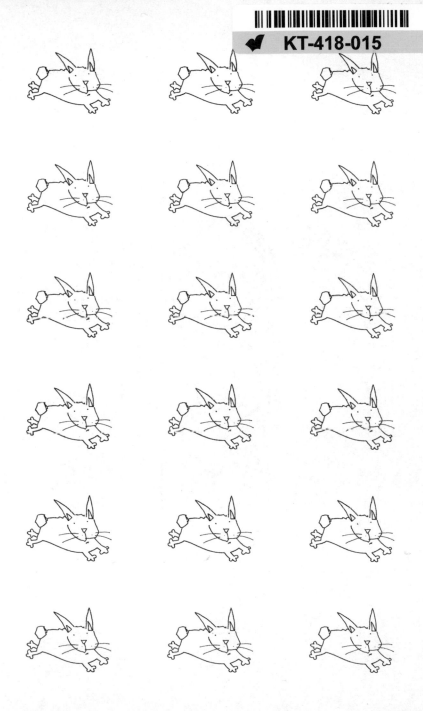

NO EYES BUT MINE
MUST READ THIS BOOK

So do not try
to sneak a look.
You have been warned!

DON'T READ!
JUST GO!

Or you might learn
things you don't
want to know.

THIS BOOK BELONGS TO

Finch Olive Penny
51 Nelson Street
Fletchley
England

AGE WHEN I STARTED THIS BOOK OF MY LIFE
Eleven years, eleven months and three weeks

MY FAMILY
Mum: Deborah Ann Penny, known as Debbie
Dad: Tom Kellogg (died before I was born)
Gran: (adopted), Olive Marie McKay, known as Nolly

BEST FRIENDS
Graeme Penny
51, Nelson Street
Fletchley

Because
* He understands exactly how I'm feeling.
* I tell him my deepest secrets – things I wouldn't tell anyone else (even Cassie).
* He never lets me down.
* He makes me laugh.

Cassandra Jane Owens, known as Cassie
3, Acacia Gardens
Fletchley

Because
* We have been friends since we were three.
* We have the same sense of humour.
* We tell each other everything (almost).
* We look after each other.
* We are dead opposites which makes it more interesting.

Nolly said *there's nothing more annoying than finding someone has doodled all over a person's newspaper. (Personally, I thought the Queen looked much more friendly with a bunny on her head.) So she gave me this notebook to doodle in instead. But I've told her it's far too nice for doodling in. I'm going to use it to record my life, hopes, etc.*

She said, **'Well, if ye write as much as ye natter, lass, ye'll be needing more than one wee book.'** *(She talks like that because she's Scottish.)*

My head is stuffed with thoughts I keep meaning to write down. And things that are personal and I don't want everyone to know. Not even my best friend Cassie. But it'll have to wait because I'm late for Cassie's. She is being slowly and painfully nagged to death about the state of her bedroom and I promised I'd help sort it for her.

Then I shall begin...

MY LIFE AND SECRET THOUGHTS
by the one and only
FINCH PENNY!

Monday, 21st June

What a yukky start to my book — did
something totally disgusting and embarrassing
at Cassie's yesterday. I threw up all over her
bedroom carpet! I think her Snoopy slippers
got a bit of a splattering too. One minute I
was trying to reach a couple of mugs under
her bed, then...EEEEUGH! Next thing I was in
the back of Cassie's mum's car, sitting on a
bin liner and clutching a bucket. Actually,
Cassie's mum was quite nice about the sick.
Usually she's Queen of the Fusspots. She's
always wiping and spraying and niggling about
things, like, *Is that a spot on your chin,
Cassie? Where's that Clearasil I bought you?*
And, *Oh, do stand up straight, Cassandra!*
Or, *I thought we were going to try and cut
down on the biscuits, darling.* It makes
Cassie dead moody.

Now I'm propped up in bed with a bucket at the ready, trying to take my mind off my insides. Mum's at work today. She's a care assistant at Greytiles Home for Wrinklies. (Home for The Elderly, really.) So Nolly's looking after me.

This is Nolly's house. Mum, me and Graeme have the flat downstairs and Nolly lives upstairs. Nolly was dead chuffed when I was born because Mum made her my adopted gran. Nolly never had children of her own. Her real name is Olive McKay, but I couldn't say Nanna Olive when I was little – it came out sounding like Nolly. Even Mum calls her that now. I don't know what happened to Mr McKay. I asked her once and all she would say was, *Dinna ask, lass. Guid riddance to the old ******!* and said a very rude word.

And that's how I got my middle name, as in Finch Olive Penny. I think Finch is a brilliant name. Of course you always get the saddos who think it's hilarious to make pathetic jokes. E.g. Bird-brain, Big Bird, Tweety-Pie, Beaky, Hop-it, etc. So I laugh it off, or flap my wings or threaten to peck their little worm-size brains out. In the Infants, Cassie used to sit on anyone who took the mickey.

Mum called me Finch because just after I was born, as she was holding me, a chaffinch landed on the hospital window ledge and sat there, peering in at me. Mum says it was as if she'd come to say hello and welcome me to the world. Mum looked down at my feathery brown hair and bright little eyes, and right there named me Finch, after that little bird.

Hold on, Graeme wants to see what I'm writing. He's a bit miffed because I haven't written anything about him yet. Don't worry, Graeme – as if I'd leave *you* out! Here's your very own write-up.

GRAEME THE GREAT
Graeme is Scottish for Graham. He'll be four in August. I'm planning a surprise party. Even though he doesn't say a lot, he's an excellent listener and seems to know exactly what I'm

thinking. He snuggles up, all ears, with this really sympathetic expression. His favourite TV programme is *Teletubbies*. He's the most intelligent rabbit I know. He's not just a garden bunny, he's a house bunny too. His best friend (next to me) is Smiffy the guinea pig next door who comes to play sometimes. This is what he looks like.

Squeak

Just been sick again, but as Nolly says, *Dinna worry, hen – better oot than in!* I like being called *hen*. It's as if I'm in a cosy nest with Mother Hen clucking over me. Nolly reminds me of a hen – small, round, fluffy and always bustling about. Except that hens don't smoke and Nolly does – *far* too much. I'm very worried about it. She could get cancer or something. I saw a programme on telly about it where they showed you some lungs full of black gunge.

I told

This is where my insides **erupted!**

Tuesday, 22nd June

I've been explodingly ill! Mum was up and down all night with me and my intestines. She got worried because I started rambling during the night about floods and jumping into lifeboats. So she phoned the surgery before she left for work. Now Nolly and I are waiting for the doctor. The stupid thing is I'm feeling a lot better now.

I think my brain was hallucinating about floods because of the washing machine. Mum put it on when she got home from work but it started gushing all over the kitchen floor. She was in a total panic till I remembered you have to turn off the little blue tap at the side. Then I was sick and needed to go to the loo, which was quite tricky managing both at the same time. Then we ran out of toilet paper which was even more tricky, so Mum zoomed off to the Co-op to get some more. She came back with the toilet rolls and a man in blue overalls. She said he was going to take a look at the washing machine for us and wasn't that nice of him?

He managed to sort it and got it working again. Mum was really pleased. So was I – until she told me she'd found him on her way to the Co-op. He was up a ladder, painting the outside of number seventeen and she'd shouted up to ask him if he knew anything about washing machines. After all she's told me about not talking to strange men! He could be a complete weirdo. I worry about Mum sometimes. She is not as sensible as me. She said he was a bargain as all he cost was a cup of coffee and she's only got twenty pounds to last the rest of the week. She forgot to mention he finished off all the biscuits in the tin.

1.50. Still waiting for the doctor. Nolly's let Graeme come in to help stop me from getting bored. He's playing Hide 'n' Seek under my bed at the moment.

2.20. Dr Khan's just left. I felt a teensy-weensy bit guilty as I was feeling OK by then, so I faked some groans when he felt my tummy. Maybe I overdid it because I could see Nolly behind him, trying to keep a straight face. It does ache a *little* bit from all that throwing up. He says I've had a

particularly nasty and **VIROOLENT** bug that's
going round. I have to
drink lots of water.
Here is my artistic
impression of the bug.

   All the while, Graeme
was taking a great interest
in the doctor's bag – and decided
to hop inside it! Dr Khan nearly walked off
with him until I told him he had a stowaway.
He looked very surprised when Graeme's little
head popped up. Dr Khan started sniffing
inside his bag suspiciously – as if Graeme
might have left a souvenir behind or
something. I assured him that Graeme is
perfectly house-trained and wouldn't dream of
doing a poo in his bag because he has his
own personal litter tray under my desk.
   Suddenly, I had this brainwave. I said,
'Doctor, could you give me some advice,
please? I have a friend who is smoking a lot.
He said, *They sound far too young to be*
smoking – do their parents know? I told him
that this person was over sixteen and an
orphan, and their adopted family are worried.
   He said you can't *make* someone give up,

they have to *want* to. He joked, *You could try telling them it's not nice to go round smelling like an old ashtray.* Then he listed some of the illnesses it causes like heart disease, strokes, etc.

I was looking hard at Nolly, hoping she'd get the message. But she started humming to herself and straightening the bed. Then she got one of her coughing fits and had to sit down. I had to explain that Nolly was the friend I'd been talking about. I could tell he was shocked. He asked her about her cough and when she last saw a doctor, which was 1978! He told her to make an appointment for a check-up. After he'd left, Graeme and me told her we had to do *something* because we love her and we're worried. And d'you know what she said? *I need a ciggie, lass.* You'd think a seventy-two-year-old would have more sense.

Mum says she doesn't know where she'd be if it wasn't for Nolly. She helped Mum through some horrible and tragic times. Like my dad dying before I was born. She doesn't know where she'd be without me, either. Even though I'm a bossy-boots. I've had plenty of practice from when I was little. Mum was

going through her bad-sad days then. Sometimes
I had to drag her out of bed in the mornings
and nag her into getting dressed. I used to put
her make-up on for her. I loved doing that.
She must have looked like one of the Addams
Family. She laughs about it now. She hasn't
had bad-sad days for ages.

Mum says I've got my dad's face and dark
brown hair. From his photo it looks like I've
got his long skinny body and legs too. I don't
take after Mum at all. She's small and fair.
And I'm nearly 2 cms taller than her!

Cassie came to see me after school with a
packet of fruit gums but I couldn't face them
so she scoffed the lot. She demonstrated her
kissing technique that she's been practising.
Not on boys – only on her arm. She showed
me three styles   (1) pecky;
                    (2) pouty;
                    (3) slobbery.

Her only real kissing experience was at
Leah's party when we were playing Murder
in the Dark and Colin Bigsby landed her a
smacker on the lips. He stank of pickled
onions and she was nearly sick. Boys of our
age are so infantile.

Wednesday, 23rd June

Back to school. Miss Phipps had a weird mark on her neck. A note went round the class saying **miss pipps got a luv byt**. It was in Shane Ripley's writing. Miss Phipps found the note and got angry with all of us because of the laughing. She made Shane stay in at breaktime. He was supposed to get the room ready for Art and cover the desks with newspaper which he did all right, but he used all the page three girls. Typical. The usual boys making immature remarks, e.g. Neil sniggering, *Cor! This one looks just like Miss*, which Miss Phipps heard and got in a very bad mood that we all had to suffer for the rest of the day.

Cassie came round after school again. She's a bit down because her parents had a HUGE row last night. She thinks it was about her. The painter man in blue overalls called while she was here. He thought he'd accidentally left his screwdriver behind. It was down the side of the washing machine. Then he asked if Mum was around. She hadn't got back from work but I lied that she was upstairs with Nolly. He could be a part-time criminal, casing the joint –

you can't trust anyone these days. I've learnt a lot from watching *The Bill* and *Crimewatch*. I certainly wouldn't have let him in if Nolly hadn't been home. Cassie says he looks just like an Action Man doll. Her brother Leo has loads of them. Cassie's right – he's got the same bristly black hair and swivelly little eyes. We couldn't stop giggling.

I think Mum is beginning to see that I was right about not inviting strange men into the house. She was quite rattled when I told her that he'd called at the flat while she was out.

Mum keeps trying to peek over my shoulder. *Always scribbling in that book of yours*, she said. *What on earth do you find to write about?*

You'd be surprised, I said.

I'm going to have to be *very* careful not to leave this book lying around. Mum can be dead nosy. And she's always popping into my room to borrow things. Which reminds me – she still hasn't given me back my pink skirt, from when she and the other care assistants at Greytiles dressed up as Spice Girls for old Alf Cobbley's hundredth birthday.

I'm hiding this book in my old *Blue Peter* jigsaw box, with all my other secret stuff –

wish lists, poems, etc. I know for certain that Mum could not resist peeping if she found it. That's how she read my last wish list which I accidentally left on my bed. She said she didn't, but how come she knew I was worried about my chest not growing? I *know* she read it, because she folded the paper up wrongly when she put it back.

Cassie and I have decided on trousers not skirts for our new uniform at Fletchley High School next term.

Thursday, 24th June

Miss Phipps wore a scarf round her neck today!

Mum came home in a really good mood. She'd been to the market and bought a lovely blue dress for herself for only £7.99 and for me a brilliant black top which was only £1.50. I love it!

She says I might have upset Nolly, because although she won't admit it, she's very nervous of doctors and hospitals. I feel bad about that so I made an excellent *SORRY NOLLY!* card. I cut out a picture of Sean Connery from the *TV Times* (he's her number one pin-up) and gave him a speech bubble like this:

Hello there, Nolly!
Finch says she's sorry-
But please take heed
And give up the weed!
Your lungs will be reborn
with lots of love
Sean
XXXXXX

I took
it up to her
and gave her a
big hug and told
her she doesn't
smell anything like an old ashtray (though she
does a bit). She said noone else would make a
card like that. I've told her I'm going to help
her all I can to cut down smoking, and if she
likes I'll go to the doctor with her and hold
her hand. She's promised to try. I'm putting
Nolly right at the top of my new wish list.

☆ ☆ Wish List ☆ ☆

1. *I wish Nolly would stop smoking.*
The SMOKING IS KILLING YOU poster that I
stuck to her kitchen door a few weeks ago
didn't do the trick. Nolly said it dropped off
and got sucked up in the hoover. Ha! As if I'd

fall for that. She just does not want to face the facts. I wish I could find ways to make her give up. She is a nicotine addict!

2. *I wish that Cassie and I are in the same class at Fletchley High School next term.*
We've filled in forms saying who we'd like to be with, but teachers can be very cunning. It's just the sort of information they use to make sure friends are *not* together. We have always been together. Ever since I was three and we met up in the Wendy House at playgroup! She was putting the dolls to bed and I was sorting out the toy plates that Shane Ripley had been using as Frisbees. We are inseparable.

3. *I wish that Mum wins the lottery.*
We are always broke. It would be brilliant to have a car and holidays and everything we dream about, and for Nolly, a luxury caravan at Swanage that she's always wanted.

4. *I wish I would stop growing. I am turning into a beanpole.*

5. *I wish my legs didn't look like sticks of celery.*

6. *I wish I didn't have to wear glasses.*

7. I wish I had some bosoms like Cassie. Well – perhaps not *that* big. She hates them. That's why she doesn't stand up straight, wears baggy jumpers and folds her arms a lot.

8. I wish that Shane Ripley will not be in the same class as me and Cassie next term at Fletchley High School.

ON MY LAST WISH LIST TWO THINGS CAME TRUE!

One, Graeme's sore paw got better and two, my nose has not grown any bigger.

Mum's friend Carol is here. She's cut Mum's hair really short and bleached it. It looks a bit punky to me but it suits her. It would look horrendous on me. I'd look like an overgrown loo brush.

Friday, 25th June

8.10. The bath is full of little hairs where Mum's been shaving her legs. She says she's fed up with looking scruffy so has decided to wear her new blue dress. Most of the time she just wears baggy old T-shirts and jeans. But when she's dressed up with her make-up on, like this morning, she looks amazing.

4.05. Came top in Maths test!

4.30. Cleaned the bath, hoovered and tidied up. Think I might have hoovered up one of Mum's socks. I found my pink skirt under a pile on her chair. It had jelly on it.

I'm a born sorter and tidy-upper. It's a good job I am because Mum isn't. We go really well together. She says the last thing she feels like when she gets home after looking after all the wrinklies at Greytiles is housework. When I was 'just a wee thing' Mum's nickname for me was *My little alien from the planet Neat.* My favourite games were sorting out the cutlery drawer and tidying the kitchen cupboards. She doesn't know how I came to be the way I am. She says my dad wasn't like this either.

5.15. Watched a programme on telly about brain surgery. It was really interesting. Made my packed lunch for tomorrow — marmalade sandwiches as nothing else in the cupboard. I am starving. Nothing left except Alphabetti Spaghetti and only 6p in the money jar. Graeme wants to play Sniff and Dig (see G for Games at back of notebook) so I shall sign off.

6.05. Mum came home with some fish and chips – and the Action Man painter! I cannot believe it after all I said about him. He wasn't wearing his overalls. I was dying to tell her about the Maths test but couldn't get a word in edgeways. I know she could tell by the look on my face what I was thinking, because she suddenly started rabbiting on about how she'd noticed him loading his van on her way to the chip shop and thought it'd be a nice way for *both* of us to say thank you for his help. She made it worse by making a joke that as everything we have is falling apart she thought he might come in useful again. He laughed. Creep.

I could see his eyes swivelling around the kitchen at the wonky cupboard doors. They nearly went into orbit when she switched the kettle on and the lights flickered.

I've been telling Mum about that dodgy
electric socket for ages. He said she ought to
have it seen to – pronto. He insisted on
doing the washing up *and* he wiped the
worktops down. His eyes kept swivelling at
her too. Later I gave Mum a right rollicking
about inviting him as we know nothing about
him. I told her I think he fancies her! I'm
dead suspicious about his screwdriver left
behind accidentally-on-purpose. She said I'd
make a good detective. I told her to be
careful or he'll get the idea *she* fancies *him*.
Ha ha ha!

Saturday, 26th June

9.10. I AM TOTALLY DEVASTATED! CASSIE
HAS JUST PHONED WITH **TERRIBLE
TERRIBLE** NEWS. We cannot believe it! She
was blubbing so much I couldn't hear what
she was saying at first.

Her mum has announced that she doesn't
want Cassie to go to Fletchley High! She
wants her to go to St Monica's School for
Girls! Where girls are *s-t-r-e-t-c-h-e-d* and
expected to apply themselves. Cassie thinks St
Monica's was what her mum and dad's huge
row was about the other day. Her mum has

arranged an interview for Cassie on Tuesday
– without even asking her first! Cassie says
the pictures in the school brochure show lots
of snooty girls playing hockey and stuff. How
could her mum do this to us?

I'm going round to Cassie's to try and
cheer her up. She is up and down a lot these
days. It's her hormones. Her periods started
ages ago. My hormones are not so active. WE
HAVE GOT TO DO SOMETHING! BUT WHAT?

Sunday, 27th June

Slept over at Cassie's last night. Our Saturday
nights at home are much more cosy than
theirs. They are never allowed to eat in front
of the telly, not even at weekends. Her mum
says it kills conversation. It doesn't kill it in
our house. It gives us all sorts of things to
talk about, like our Let's-Pretend-We've-
Won-The-Lottery game. Anyway, Cassie's
dad read his paper all the way through the
meal which I think is very bad manners. And
her annoying little brother Leo kept count of
every single potato Cassie ate (nine).

Cassie and I are distraught about St
Monica's. She lay lifelessly on her bed wailing,
I'm not going. I refuse to go. She can't make

me. *She'll have to drag me there. Anyway, Dad doesn't want me to – he says it's a waste of money.*

It got really boring so I starting sorting her room at last. I found her gold locket that she thought she'd lost. That cheered her up. For about thirty seconds. Then she kept interrupting with, *Don't put my hair-drier away – oh and leave my curling tongs out – put them in my bag – I'll need them when I run away. And if you find my Walkman put that in too,* etc. If she does run away, she's going to need a removal van. Then she lost interest and sat on the bed eating crisps and making unhelpful suggestions.

This Is What I Found
(among loads of other things)

1. *My* green nail varnish!
2. Cassie's Maths book which she swore to Mr
3. Buckeridge she had given in.
4. And Cassie's list of New Year resolutions, e.g.

I will tidy my room!!!

I will cut down on crisps and chocolate.

I will be more patient with Leo.

(Scratched out in a mad frenzy with red marker pen.)

28

I made an excellent job of it. CDs and cassettes in alphabetical order. Comics and mags stacked. Desk cleared and papers filed in folders. Bits and bobs sorted into pots. Pinboard rearranged under headings, and three bin bags full of rubbish! I might be an interior designer one day.

When Cassie's mum saw her room she hugged me and called me a wonder! Which made me feel like a traitor because: (a) I am furious with her about St Monica's and (b) it wasn't nice for Cassie.

Then Cassie bellowed at her, *You might be interested to know that I'm seriously thinking about running away!*

Her mum said, *Before or after supper, Cassie dear? I wouldn't want to waste a perfectly good pork chop if you're not going to be here.*

The weird thing is, sometimes I think Cassie's mum likes *me* more than Cassie. On parents' evening, right in front of Cassie, she told my mum how lucky she was to have me and how she couldn't understand how she herself could have produced such a couldn't-care-less daughter like Cassandra! If only she would *apply* herself more then she could easily achieve As on her school report too and not all those disappointing Ds and Es. That's not very nice, is it?

We managed to take our minds off things a bit by going through some of Cassie's old mags and drawing in some cosmetic surgery on those sickeningly perfect smug girl models. Cassie did a brilliant one with hairy warts, crossed eyes, missing teeth, spots and blackheads, and underneath wrote,

OUR LOVELY MODEL, SOPHIE,
THE FACE OF THE MILLENNIUM.

When I got home the Action Man was fixing our dodgy kitchen socket. Mum and him were killing themselves laughing over something. Then he started nattering to me about music and asking what groups I like. I hate it when adults try and act young. He must be at least thirty-seven! I hope he realises he's wasting his time if he fancies Mum. Though she was really going over the top about how grateful she was *and* she'd bought some cans of beer. She couldn't really fancy him, could she? No! Yukkety-yuk!

  Wish List continued

9. I wish that Cassie does not get into St

Monica's as she does not want to go and it is all her mum's idea. She would be totally miserable there.

Cassie and I are going to chant, *We wish, we wish, that Cassie goes to Fletchley High School,* three times a day (at least), at 12.30, 4 o'clock and 9 o'clock, twenty times minimum, preferably out loud but, otherwise in our heads.

At bedtime I asked Mum if she fancies the Action Man. She laughed, *Look – he's just trying to do us a few favours. I like him for that – and I'm very grateful. It's no big deal, OK?*

TOMORROW IS MY 12TH BIRTHDAY!

Monday, 28th June

HAPPY BIRTHDAY TO ME!
YES! TODAY I AM **TWELVE!!!**
Mum woke me up early before she left for work. I was a bit disappointed because she gave me an itsy-bitsy envelope and said, *It's all I could manage, love – money's a bit tight at the moment.*

Inside was a slip of paper. It said, Clue 1:
THE WETTER I GET THE MORE I DRY. She'd
made up a treasure hunt! Ha! That was easy.
I ran into the bathroom and there on my
towel was another clue. It said, Clue 2: TEA –
MILK AND ONE SUGAR PLEASE, Love Nolly.

So I took a cup of tea up to Nolly and she
gave me another clue, till about six clues
later – inside Nolly's tumble drier – I
found...a pair of rollerblades! I couldn't
believe it! Now I won't have to borrow
Cassie's. They must have cost a bomb. It will
take Mum ages to pay them off from the
catalogue. I've been saving up but I've only
got £7.84 so far. Graeme gave me some
vanilla bubble bath. Got eleven cards. Nine of
them have rabbits on them.

Twelve feels so much older and different to
eleven. I don't know why. I keep looking at
myself in the mirror but I don't *look* any
different. I was hoping my chest might have
grown a bit with all that arm-swinging I've
been doing. It's *still* only 75.8 cm. Cassie's is
enormous – she's been wearing bras for ages,
but she is nearly thirteen.

Have to go to school now. I'm inviting
Carmen, Kayleigh, Sarah and Leah to my party

on Friday. And Cassie of course. I'll take votes today on whether to have pizza or pasta.

At school Cassie gave me a beautiful silver chain with a bird on it. She says it's a finch. I wore it under my school shirt but Miss Phipps made me take it off in games. Shane Ripley made a stupid joke in front of everyone that he'd heard I had a bird inside my shirt and was it a little tit? I could have died! But I told him everyone knew what was inside his shirt. A great twit! Ho ho!

Nolly gave me a book about rabbits with pictures of the most adorable little bunnies. Read some to Graeme about the rabbit that weighed 11.4 kilos. His eyes almost popped out. Also she made the most amazing birthday cake in the shape of a pair of rollerblades! We are saving it till my party on Friday.

The rollerblades are magic. It's the closest you can get to flying. Cassie's teaching me how to do turns. Mum came out and had a go on them too. I had quite a job getting them back. Sometimes I feel I'm more grown up than she is.

I think she's making up for her lost childhood.
The trouble is she was only just seventeen
when she had me. That's only five years older
than I am! Far too young if you ask me. I'm
not sure if I shall have children. I have other
plans. Actually, after that programme I saw
on telly, a brain surgeon sounds quite
interesting. It's just the sort of job that
would need someone who is neat and careful
and good at remembering exactly where
everything goes. I bet there aren't many
women brain surgeons.

Tuesday, 29th June

Mum had a letter from the bank this morning.
She is £481.01 overdrawn. She says she doesn't
have to be told. She knows. Right down to
the last penny. And the last thing she needs is
to be charged £25 extra for sending her a
letter to remind her. I gave her my £7.84
that I'd saved for rollerblades and the £5
Boots token that Auntie Moira sent me for
my birthday. Mum's eyes went all watery.

Cassie's not at school as she was visiting
the awful St Monica's. Loads of people
away because of The Viroolent Bug. Not
Shane Ripley. He is never ill unfortunately –

even germs can't stand him. Went around with Kayleigh and Carmen. They were going to have skirts for uniform but I persuaded them into trousers. We have to stick together at our new school.

4.10. Cassie phoned and started to tell me how awful St Monica's was but her irritating brother Leo picked up the phone and started going *Hello, Bird-brain! Tweet-tweet-tweet!* He's like a wind-up toy. Anyway, Cassie clobbered Leo, so he started screaming – then her mum had a go at Cassie! I could hear it all going on in the background. Cassie will tell all tomorrow. She sounded dead miz. She told me that St Monica's costs **£2,400 a term!** Mum laughed hysterically when I told her. We could think of loads more interesting things to spend it on! Mum chose a villa in Greece with its own pool, I chose Disney World and Nolly fancies the Italian Lakes. Cassie's dad must earn loads of money from selling all those conservatories.

Nolly says she has cut down to fifteen ciggies a day but I found twenty-one butts in her pedal bin! (Which I know for a fact she empties every morning.) She says it's like living with Sherlock Holmes. Mum is right. I would make an excellent detective.

Wednesday, 30th June

Cassie LOATHED St Monica's. It's full of posh, frightfully polite, clever girls who have ponies. She seemed a *tiny* bit more cheerful because she's sure she won't get in. She deliberately did everything she could think of to put them off wanting her, like slouching and yawning. When the headmistress asked her what her ambitions were, she said to have lots of babies, which is true. Her mum was furious. The only thing that Cassie liked was the heated indoor swimming pool. The uniform makes all the girls look like Toad of Toad Hall. She thinks it's completely unnatural to have only girls and no boys. She is always drooling about boys. She fancies Leah's brother, but he's seventeen – no chance! Personally, I think that all girls and no boys is brilliant.

Cassie helped with my new poster for Nolly. It's excellent. This is what it looks like.

Five Good Reasons for Giving Up Smoking

1. Your home will smell of fresh air instead of stale smoke.
2. You will not cough your lungs up every morning.
3. Your food will taste much better and you won't have to put salt all over it which is bad for you too.
4. You will save lots of money on ciggies and air freshener.
5. You will not be harming me, Mum and Graeme with passive smoking. COUGH-COUGH!

YOU CAN DO IT NOLLY!

We stuck it on her fridge door and lent her my old Little Miss Neat money box for all the money she saves. At last she has promised to try to cut down to ten a day. It's a start, I suppose, but she can be a right fibber sometimes so I will keep an eye on her.

Thursday, 1st July

Mum was dead ratty this morning because Graeme chewed her only pair of tights. Well, she shouldn't leave them on the floor. Her room looks like a jumble sale. If it wasn't for me this place would be a tip. I just hope Graeme's intestines will not be knotted up with black lycra.

For homework Miss Phipps says we all have to write an essay about ourselves which will be given to our new teachers at Fletchley High. Started my essay but interrupted twice by Action Man painter on the phone asking for Mum. Private Detective Finch Penny's suspicions were correct. He *does* fancy her.

5.25. Mum just rang to say she is doing some overtime and won't be back till 6.30.
I will welcome her with one of my fry-ups!

6.40. Mum arrived home with the Action Man! AGAIN! He was dressed in a casual outfit. He brought some Chinese takeaway. Fry-up completely wasted. Even Graeme turned his nose up at it. Afterwards, the Action Man fetched his toolbox and fixed all the kitchen cupboards.

⊙K. It was nice to see Mum looking so chuffed — she kept opening and shutting all the doors. Yes, I admit it — those cupboards have been driving us both mad. One door kept falling off. And I know that Nolly's noisy radiators sometimes sound like a herd of dying dinosaurs and it's great he's going to take a look at them for her. BUT...I am VERY suspicious. A handyman friend would be very useful but he's here nearly every day! And he acts like he owns the place. I caught him helping himself to biscuits again – all the chocolate ones. I do not think he is a criminal any more but he *definitely* fancies Mum. His eyes were swivelling like crazy. Does his wife know?

Fried egg floating in the loo and it won't flush away.

Friday, 2nd July
7.30 a.m. THE VERY WORST THING HAS HAPPENED! I CANNOT BEAR IT! CASSIE IS GOING TO ST MONICA'S! She just phoned – they got a letter from St Monica's offering her a place! It said they not only welcome high achievers but the qualities of **Caring for Others** and **Doing Your Best**. Then Leo picked up the extension, so Cassie screamed that *he'd* better take care because she was going

to do *her* best to murder him, the obnoxious little monster!

I couldn't eat any breakfast. I'm too distraught. Nolly said, *Dinna worry, lass, it's not as if she's going to Australia.* Mum said it's Cassie she feels sorry for. What about me! Thank goodness I have Graeme. He's sitting on the bed with me, licking my toes which is very comforting. My party tonight. Definitely need cheering up!

11.00 p.m. Brilliant! Had lasagne and watched *Titanic*. Cried loads. Got luminous Yo-Yo from Carmen, *Temptation* body spray and talc from Kayleigh, nail varnish set from Leah and a box with a rabbit on it from Sarah.

More **Wishes** For List

10. I wish that Cassie's mum realises how mean and bossy she is and how unhappy she is making Cassie by sending her to St Monica's and changes her mind. PLEASE! PLEASE!

11. If that doesn't work, I wish that some disaster befalls St Monica's, e.g. catching fire or a minor earthquake so it disappears into a hole in the ground, then Cassie can go to the school that she wants – Fletchley High, with me! She

will be so lonely and miserable at St Mon's.
P.S. *I wish no one gets hurt in the disaster.*

Saturday, 3rd July
8.45. Mum at work, doing more overtime to pay off the bills.
Washing-up from party still in sink.
Rang Cassie — left message on answerphone.

9.30. Kind, generous and thoughtful daughter and friend Graeme decide to surprise mother when she gets home from Greytiles Home with:
1. A pile of nice clean washing
2. A shiny clean flat

11.40. Nice clean washing hanging on line.

12.35. Kind daughter, alias Private Detective F. Penny and her tracker-bunny Graeme find suspicious evidence in dustbin, when emptying pedal bin, of a mystery visitor! Found:
a) Leftovers of takeaway chicken tikka masala, rice, poppadums, etc. **FOR TWO!!!** And a receipt from A Taste of India for Saturday 26th June!!! The night of daughter's sleepover at friend Cassie's, when mother said

she didn't mind being on her own, when daughter felt guilty leaving her mother all lonesome.

b) Also, empty wine bottle and two beer cans. (Mother hates beer. Mrs Olive McKay of same address only likes sherry, whisky and ginger wine.)

c) Plus an empty Ben and Jerry Chunky Monkey ice-cream tub.

Who was the mystery visitor? Why was daughter not told?

12.45. Visit Mrs Olive McKay upstairs to enquire who the mystery visitor was but she was no help at all as she was out at Bingo with her friend Betty Barnstaple on the night in question.

16.10. Mother steps through back door and is shown evidence on kitchen table of Indian takeaway for two. Daughter wants to know who mysterious visitor was. Mother thinks this is funny and says it's not a criminal offence. Daughter says, *Why hide the evidence, then?*

   She confessed then. Just as I thought – it

was the **Action Man!** She invited him! She's been meeting up with him after work AND during her lunch breaks too! I am very angry and very upset. Why the big secret then? Why didn't she tell me this from the start? What was all that about, *It's no big deal. I'm just grateful*, stuff? We NEVER lie to each other.

She says she didn't lie to me. That's how it was — to start with. She waffled on about how she grew to like him more but needed to be absolutely sure that he wasn't some big phoney. She wouldn't let herself think about it too much in case it didn't work. Also, she was a bit nervous about telling me in case I didn't like him. Too right. In fact she was going to tell me today because he's invited us to The Pizza Place this evening and then to the pictures.

I said, *No way, it's good telly tonight. And what about our lottery game? And what if he's got a wife or a girlfriend you don't know about?*

She said he hasn't got a girlfriend and he's divorced. I told her that he couldn't be much good if no one wanted him except *her*. She snorted, *Now you can see why I didn't want*

to tell you, Miss Bossy-Boots! and went off to
have a shower.

*And what about his kids? I bet they'll be
pleased, ha ha! I do not think so!* I shouted
through the shower curtain. He doesn't have
any. That's why they're divorced. His wife
didn't want any kids and he did. How could
Mum know all this about him and never tell
me? I yelled, *Well, he's blooming well not
having ME!* She yelled back that he wouldn't
blooming well want me if I was going to be
so revolting.

I went bananas then. She didn't even notice
the shiny clean flat or the nice neat pile of
washing or anything. So I stomped up to
Nolly's, then remembered she'd gone shopping
so I sat at the top of the stairs, crying. Mum
came up and said she was sorry about not
telling me straight away and calling me
revolting. Flipping well should be too. She
hugged me and said anyone would be mad not
to want me because I'm amazing. Even
Cassie's mum likes me and she's dead fussy.

I said I just hoped Action Man wasn't
anything like the horrid Ray Beasley. She said
she didn't think I'd remember him. Oh, yes
I do. Even though I was only four and a bit.

I reminded her that I didn't like him either –
and I was right as it turned out. Which
proves I am a much better judge of character
than she is.

She says the Action Man is nothing like
Ray Beasley. He's kind and gentle. She could
tell straight away by his eyes. I think they're
sneaky, swivelly eyes. She wants me to be my
usual nice friendly self tonight. I don't see
why I should. Not after all the trouble he's
caused. Mum and me hardly ever argue. And
she's never kept secrets from me. Never ever.
He isn't just a handyman friend. He's a
BOYFRIEND! And I can't stand him.

10.15 p.m. His name is Ian Tanner. He kept
calling Mum, Debs. Cringe-making. Everyone
calls her Debbie. I was very very polite. *Yes,
thank you. How kind of you, Mr Tanner.
Terribly sorry but I can't manage this pizza,
I'm not that hungry, actually.*

I made not one mention of
his eyes swivelling away at
Mum. At the pictures I made
sure I sat in the middle and insisted
on popcorn. And a Kingcone. When we got
back Mum kept hinting how it was time for

me to go to bed. I reminded her that she always lets me stay up late on Saturdays. Four nil to me. Neat.

Sunday, 4th July
Went round to Cassie's. It's not fair! I WANT TO GO TO ST MONICA'S! IT IS TOTALLY UTTERLY **BRILLIANT!**

Cassie showed me the school brochure. She is mad not to want to go there!

Here are
MY TEN REASONS WHY I WANT TO GO.
St. Monica's has:

1. Eighty acres of woods and hills and beautiful gardens where girls can stroll and have picnics or go riding!
2. The most luscious library!
3. Truly exceptional exam results!
4. The most stunning science and technology labs!
5. A real theatre!
6. Its very own pet house! Graeme would love it!
7. The most astounding art studio I have ever seen!
8. An incredible indoor heated swimming pool!

9. *The opportunity for the able pupil (me) to excel academically in pursuit of her chosen career whether sportswoman, artist, musician, businesswoman or Prime Minister. (Me!)*
10. Hundreds of hobbies and activities! Drama, riding, canoeing...

I think I started to dribble when I saw the photos in the brochure. And Cassie was whinging, *I'm going to hate it, I know I am! Look at all those smug-looking girls! They'll all be sporty and brainy and I'll be thick! It's a waste of money sending me there! That's what Dad said.*

I was thinking, But it wouldn't be wasted on *me!* I'd LOVE it. Cos IT IS **PERFECT** FOR ME! AND I AM **PERFECT** FOR IT!

I couldn't stop raving on about it. *You don't know how lucky you are, Cassie! Tell you what – I'll swap places with you!*

She went all moody. *Some friend you are! I thought you wanted us to stay together!*

So I said, *OK – you take the Action Man and I'll take St Mon's. And you'll be my friend for ever and ever!*

I tried telling her about my horrible weekend with the A. Man but she just kept moaning and groaning and wailing about how her mum won't listen to her and how even her best friend (me) is no help! It's not fair! I'd give anything to go to a place like St Mon's, yet all she does is whine. And it *will* be wasted on Cassie. Why should she get to go there? I'm much more '*able*' than she is! I'd LOVE '*to excel academically*' in my chosen career! You could stretch Cassie till her brains squeaked but she'd never excel academically. Her dad's right. It's a waste of money. I'm not being nasty. **It's true!**

I raced home, bursting to tell Mum about St Mon's. She was snuggled up on the settee with the Action Man when I got back, showing him our photo albums. It was open at one of me sitting on my potty!

I pretended he wasn't there. When I'd finished telling her all about it, she laughed. *It sounds fantastic, love – I'll ask for a pay rise, then, shall I?*

Then the Action Man said, *You know, Finch, if people really cared about education, they'd be supporting their local schools and demanding the best for everyone. Come on – you don't really think it's right that only rich kids should get the best, do you?*

I believe he should mind his own business,

so I told him, *No. That's why I want to go there! I'll show them that poor kids can get all those amazing exam results too!*

He gave his know-it-all smile. *The reason they get such amazing results is because they hand-pick lots of very bright children. Anyway, Fletchley's a good school. My brother teaches there. You'll be all right there – don't worry.*

That's all I need. An Action Man spy at school. And now he's an expert on education! Then he said, *And if you fancy canoeing, well, I've got a canoe and a kayak down at the Heron Canoe Centre. I do a bit of teaching there. How about coming along and having a go? We could go this afternoon if you like.*

No thank you, Mr Tanner, I said, and me and Graeme escaped to Nolly's. I think I will make him a badge that says **THE WORLD EXPERT ON EVERYTHING.** (He's been here eight times in the last fourteen days.)

I really hate him – more than ever. I can't pretend, can I? Then Mum would think I like him. That would be the same as telling a lie.

Nolly came down to our flat this evening. She's right fidgety and grumpy and has been having weird dreams about the devil offering her boxes of cigarettes. There was this really good film I was trying watch about a girl who saves a man's life then discovers he's an escaped murderer. But the Action Man nattered all the way through about this amazing dog he had once that died. It could count up to five and do duck impressions. How it put up with Action Man I don't know.

All day long I've been thinking about St Mon's. I told Graeme all about it. His little eyes shone when I told him about the woods and hills and gardens and the pet house. It's the first time I've ever been jealous of Cassie.

  ## Wish 12.

I wish that I could go to St Monica's! It would be my dream come true! All we need is £2,400 a term! I'll give Mum a pound to do the lottery for me and win some money! **PLEASE, PLEASE,** make it happen.

I take back wish number 11 because St Monica's is too brilliant to have a disaster happen to it! I never realised there were places like that. BIG SIGH. What's Cassie whinging about? What's happening? Why is everyone getting good things and I'm getting all the rubbish?

7.40. Cassie rang to say she didn't mean the things she said. She blamed it on her hormones.

Monday, 5th July

I had a terrible nightmare that the Action Man moved in with us and used my room for his canoe. I had to sleep in a tent in the garden. Don't think about it. It's too disgustingly dreadful! I'd never let it happen. I'm going to make sure Mum knows that.

Practised for Sports Day at school. I hate sport. So does Cassie. We're in the obstacle race. I mean, what is the point? All the boys were ogling the girls' chests, especially Cassie's. She went all red and wouldn't run properly in case it bounced. We don't stand a chance.

Went round Cassie's after school. Leo was out. Hallelujah! We played silly games with Cassie's old Barbie and one of Leo's Action Men. Cassie was Barbie and I was Action Man.

BARBIE: You're not wearing that are you?
ACTION MAN: Why, what's wrong?
BARBIE: There's no way you're

	coming shopping at Tesco's in your scuba diving outfit!
ACTION MAN:	Well, you look pretty stupid in that ballgown!
BARBIE:	How dare you! This dress cost me £2.99!
ACTION MAN:	Anyway, Action Man does NOT do Tesco's. Action Man is tough. Action Man is fearless. Action Man does washing machines. And kitchen cupboards!

Then Cassie got them kissing, so I grabbed Barbie and she gave him a kung fu kick right in his zipper, and he and his snorkel went flying across the bed. We couldn't stop laughing.

Got Graeme to choose my lottery numbers. I put some numbered cards on the floor with a Cheerio

on each one. He went bonkers racing round
and nibbling. The first six he nibbled were 41,
3, 13, 24, 11, and 47.

Gave Mum £1 to buy a lottery ticket for me.
All I need is

£2,400 per term X 3 terms = £7200 per year!!
£7,200 per year X 6 years = **£43,200 !!!!!!**

WHAT!

I cannot believe it! £43,200! I suppose it's
not that much if you win £12 million or
something. Personally I'd be quite happy with
£100,000. I'd need enough for uniform, hockey
sticks, etc. And there'd still be plenty left
over for Mum and Nolly.

Wish 13.

*I wish the Action Man joins the Commandos;
gets splatted by his own toxic gunge gun; falls
off his polar mission sledge; jumps out of his
gyrocopter without a parachute; drops off his
bungee rope; and paddles his canoe right over
the rapids.*

Tuesday, 6th July
Mum has gone to Quiz Night at the King's
Head with the A. Man. We were still eating

our spaghetti when he arrived. I watched the way Mum looks at him like a puppy and laughs at all his stupid jokes. He brought me a box of Maltesers. Creep-crawly. I was super polite and acted sickeningly thrilled. I am upstairs with Nolly now. She's a bit ratty because she's used up her ration of ten ciggies. I know because I counted them. Sacrificed half my Maltesers to take her mind off smoking. I've told her she is looking much better. I wish she'd go to the doctor's and get some of those patches.

10.55. Mum just got in. She came into my room to kiss me goodnight and said, *I knew you'd like Ian once you got to know him!* WHAT!!? I could smell his disgusting aftershave on her.

Wednesday, 7th July
Lottery tonight! I WISH! I WISH! I WISH!

YES! YES! YES! I WON! I got three numbers! Ten pounds! Clever little Graeme! Tomorrow I'll buy him some grapes as a reward. He goes mad for them. You have to warm them up in your hands to make them nice and juicy. He races up and down with excitement, squeaking, *Grapes! Grapes! Goody-goody!*

Phoned Cassie and told her the good news. She's going to think up some other ways of raising money.

I know it's not £100,000 but it's a start. Mum didn't get any of her numbers. The best bit is planning how we're going to spend our fortune. We snuggle up on the settee and Mum makes up these stories about how she'd say to her Never-can-please boss Mrs Skeeting, *Now that I'm a multimillionaire, Mrs S, I'd like to tell you to stick your mingy £4.75 an hour down the toilet, also your horrible dribbling dog with the killer breath and your stingy Christmas present of six bathcubes!* Then we make up our shopping list.

1. A new house with a big garden, plus an indoor heated swimming pool and a private wildlife park with penguins and Shetland ponies for me. Also a Rabbit World Theme Park for Graeme. Mum

would really like orang-utans, but we've decided it would be cruel to keep them caged up. So we'll take a trip to Borneo and see them in the wild. She's got a thing about orang-utans. Perhaps that's why she likes the Action Man, ha ha!.

2. A white chauffeur-driven limo for Nolly and a red sports car for Mum.

3. A luxury caravan at Swanage for Nolly, just five minutes walk from the beach.

Then we'll sail away on our private yacht, reclining on our deck-loungers, sipping cocktails from those tall glasses with little umbrellas and mangoes and things floating in them. Later, we'll put on our Calvin Klein dresses and dance the night away.

Actually that last bit's Mum's. I think I'd be a bit bored with the yacht.

Now I've added:

4. Me, trotting down the posh drive of our new house in my stripy St Mon's blazer (I've decided I don't want to be a boarder), waving goodbye to Mum in her silk negligée on the balcony of our new palatial home. At

school I'll be peering down my digital microscope in the science block, brushing up on my French in the language lab, then on to the art studio, astounding everyone, including myself, with my newly discovered artistic talent, and finally, a quick canter on my pony through the woods before returning home.

Mum is good at making up stories. When I was little she'd make up the most amazing bedtime stories. My favourite was 'The Magic Bed'. She'd turn the knob on the bed and say, *Rise bed! Fly bed! Out of the window — tonight we wish to fly to Cloudland*, or 'The Mermaid Lagoon', or whatever, and she'd invent adventures. They'd go on for weeks because I'd always fall asleep.

CONGRATULATIONS GRAEME!
Only £95,990 to go!

Thursday, 8th July
The Action Man's been here all evening again. He jogs over then arrives all panting and sweaty trainers, complains he's hot and starts throwing windows open as if he owns the place. Except the windows haven't been

opened for years so he attacked them with his mighty chisel, dead pleased with himself when the arctic winds blew in and we were sitting here shivering. I don't know why Mum's so thrilled. We were perfectly ⊙K with stuck windows.

Then he was really sucking up about how delicious Mum's cooking was. It was eggs and chips for flipping sakes! He did the drying-up but put everything in the wrong place and completely messed up the cutlery drawer. Then he had the cheek to tell me that his way was more L⊙GICAL! I said it wasn't, even though I didn't know what it meant. I looked it up. All it means is sensible. Well, I think it would be logical for him to pack his kitbag and take a hike because he is invading my territory. I couldn't concentrate on my essay because of all their nattering. Did my recorder practice instead but Mum got snappy. Why should I have to practise in my room just because of him? Anyway, I'm getting fed up with my room. It's too little-girlish.

Mum just told me it's time for bed but I'm ignoring her. She was in the bathroom brushing her teeth ten minutes ago. I bet it's kissing preparation. EEUGH! You wouldn't catch me kissing him even with a surgical mask. It's a good job they can't see what I'm writing. He's got his horrible hairy arm along the settee behind her.

oh oh oh
chocolate
biscuits

Action Man, Action Man,
Arms just like an orangutan.
Why don't you just leave us, please,
And swing away through the trees?

Friday, 9th July

Gave my essay in today. It was nine pages long. I did a whole page on things I'd like to be, including what I'd do if I was Prime Minister. I've been thinking about that ever since I saw the St Mon's brochure. I think it's time some of those MPs learnt some manners. I saw them on the telly in the House of Commons, shouting and banging like hooligans. If we behaved like that in class, Miss Phipps would make us go outside, line up and come in again properly.

My essay got me thinking about my dad too. What would it have been like if he hadn't died? And what would he think of me?

I bet he'd be proud. Action Man wouldn't stand a chance. Dad's name was Tom Kellogg. All Mum's got is one photo of him. He was very good-looking with dark hair (like me), sitting on his motorbike. He was a student then. (Mum says that's where I get my brains from.) They met in the café where Mum was working and it was **LOVE AT FIRST SIGHT**. He was working on a building site during the holidays. They were saving up to go around the world on his bike, then some scaffolding fell on him and he was killed. It was so ROMANTIC and so TRAGIC.

It's no wonder she got depressed with all those bad things happening. It took a long time before she got better. Sometimes, when I was little, Mum would get so down, she'd shut herself away in the cupboard under the stairs. Then, I'd shout up the stairs, *Nolly! Mummy's under the stairs again!* Nolly would come down and be Mother Hen.

I'd sit outside, singing and talking to Mum through the door. She says that's when she learned how stubborn I could be. I'd do my Big Bad Wolf act, *If you don't come out, I'll huff and I'll puff and I'll blow the door down.*

Then I'd cheer her up with little jam sandwiches. I'd cut them into fancy shapes with my Little Cook pastry set: stars and diamonds and circles. And I'd brush her hair for her. I was three or only four or something. I wanted to be a hairdresser then.

She says that after my dad died she wanted some scaffolding to fall on her too. She'd never have managed without Nolly – Nolly ran the café that she was working in. She didn't know that she was expecting me because I was no bigger than a tadpole then. When she found out I was a BIG SHOCK. But later, when I was born, I was a **WONDERFUL SURPRISE**.

Nolly invited Mum to stay with her till she had the baby (me), and got herself sorted. And we're still here! That's how she became my adopted gran. So something good came out of it after all. ME! Tarah! And I got a gran and six adopted aunties too because Nolly's got six sisters, which is good because we don't have any other family.

Mum's parents died a year apart, so from when she was twelve she lived with an aunt and uncle. They were quite old and they didn't really want her. She hated her uncle.

He was a bully, always finding fault with her and making her feel bad. She was really unhappy there, and left at sixteen. Then she met my dad. But she never knew him long enough to find out anything about his family. Which has given me an idea. Wouldn't it be brilliant to find Nan and Grandad Kellogg? I bet they'd be thrilled to discover they've got a granddaughter! I think I might do some secret detective work.

  ## Wish 14.

I wish I can find out more about my dad and find my Nan and Grandad Kellogg and give them a big surprise. Also I wish my dad hadn't died. But it's too late for that now.

Saturday, 10th July

10.05. The Action Man just arrived with his neat shiny toolbox, ready to grapple with the radiators. He found some of Mum's bras and pants behind hers. Heard him saying he liked the black bra best. Yuk. Pass the sickbag. I had to make a difficult choice. Stay and keep my eye on them, or escape to Nolly's? Graeme said that if we hiked up to Nolly's we could sneak down and spy on them.

Spying on him draining our radiators got boring after a bit, so we helped Nolly give her Virgin Marys a bath. She's got two of them, one on her sideboard and one on her bedroom mantelpiece. This is because she is a **Roman Catholic**. She rinses them in Alpine Meadow fabric softener so they smell nice. I don't know much about Catholics except what Nolly's told me. We've only done Hindus, Diwali, Muslims, Buddhists and the Salvation Army in RE. Perhaps I was away for Catholics. This is what I know about them:

1. Their leader is the Pope.

2. They like the Virgin Mary and pray to her.

3. They go to church and do Confession. This is when they own up to the priest about their sins. I asked Nolly if she confessed about the time the Co-op gave her change for £10 instead of a £5 note, and she kept it. She snapped, *Och! Tha's between me and Father Coogan!*

4. They have priests called 'Father' someone. Nolly's is Father Coogan. He smokes even more than Nolly. He stinks of ten old ashtrays. You have to spray the hall after he's been. I think that's a very bad example when smoking costs so much. He should give up too and give the money to the poor and homeless.

I'm not sure about religion and God. Is he real or just made up to explain things we don't understand? And why is God a **HE**? It could be a **SHE**. Or a bit of both. Why don't miracles happen these days? It would save the hospitals a lot of money. Hinduism sounds quite interesting, especially about reincarnation – that's being reborn into a new life after you die. You can become a different person, an animal even. Like the

Queen could come back as an Australian aborigine or a hippopotamus. Maybe my dad is walking around right now in a new body. He might even be Graeme! Perhaps he is! Perhaps that's why we get on so well and he can read my thoughts. Hold on – I'll ask him.

He gave me a really KNOWING stare. Then he washed his ears. Does this mean something? Got Graeme to choose my lottery numbers again. The winning numbers this week are: 3, 11, 19, 25, 26, 45!

Not one measly number! We didn't play our lottery fantasy game. I wasn't going to have

the Action Man earwigging all my secret
dreams. Even worse, Graeme sat on his lap!
I gave Graeme a good talking-to. The trouble
is, he's just a big softie and he doesn't like
being rude to people. But he's got to get
tough and stand up to the enemy — not drool
all over them.

Sunday, 11th July

Q. Doesn't the Action Man have a home
   to go to?
A. Yeah. With the other apes in deepest Borneo.

Wish 15.

I JUST WISH HE'D GO THERE.

Me and Graeme have practically taken up
residence upstairs with Nolly. The A. Man
didn't even do any jobs today, just lazed
about with his CD player going non-stop. It's
worse still when he sings along. He's moved in
loads of his things — the shelves are groaning
with his tapes and CDs. If he's thinking of
moving himself in he has made a big error!

I just went downstairs to get my Yo-Yo,
and they were **KISSING!** Yuk! I was so
disgusted, but delighted to see that they

looked embarrassed and quickly pretended to be reading the papers. I said to Mum, *I just wanted to ask you about Dad. Remember him?* And told her about my essay and how I thought it'd be interesting to trace Nan and Grandad Kellogg and asked what she could remember about them. All I got was a big sigh and, *It's a long time ago, love. I don't know anything about them.* Then the Action Man tried to change the subject by showing me how to do the spaghetti trick with my Yo-Yo.

I don't even get any sympathy from Nolly which amazes me. The way she snorts and puffs about her old husband I thought she'd be more fussy. But when I was listing all Action Man's horrible habits she laughed and said, *Och! Dinna be so pickie, lass!* She says that anyone who can stop her radiators rattling and fix her fuzzy telly like he did, gets her vote. Also she thinks he looks a bit like Sean Connery. What's happening to the women in this house? Get a man in the house with a drill and a screwdriver and they're drooling. It's pathetic. I'm going to make certain I can fix things for myself. We don't need men. Not these days. You can even have babies without them. I saw a really interesting telly programme about it. I think I will pray for a miracle that the Action Man remembers where he lives which is **NOT HERE**.

I got so fed up this evening I sat in the middle of the settee and watched this totally boring programme about farming subsidies. Mum kept hinting it was time for bed so I told her I had to watch it for homework. Then she snorts, *OK! I'll record it for you!* The Action Man grins, *Let her watch it – I don't mind.* He knew I wasn't really interested – I had to prop my eyes open to stay awake. He just wanted to see me suffer. Then Mum says, *Well, I DO mind. Goodnight, Finch!* So I flounced out. There's nothing like a good flounce to make a point. And the point is Mum's in there with him and I'm sent to my room. It's like the flat's not our own any more. She prefers the Action Man to me.

00:35. He's *still* here – I heard him laughing.

00:53. He's gone at last. I hope he gets abducted by aliens on the way home and is used by them for painful experiments.

Monday, 12th July

Miss Phipps told Shane Ripley to try and write a bit more for his essay about himself but he said, *I'm not doing no more and no one can make me.* All he'd written was, **I hate shcool and stuff about myself is none of your bisness.** He said his dad told him to write that.

Went to Cassie's after school and tried to think of ways to raise money so I can go to St Mon's with her. She said if I could kidnap her brother Leo and hold him to ransom I'd be doing her two big favours in one go. Other more *useful* ideas are:

Sell some things. My rollerblades? Yes – I'm that desperate!
Make things to sell. E.g. popcorn, cakes, etc.
Do jobs for people.
Find some buried treasure (another of Cassie's ideas). Told her that sort of thing only happens in stories.

The problem is I worked out that £2,400 a term is about £200 for every school week! That's nearly as much as Mum earns! All those ideas are useless. I shall have to keep trying with the lottery.

No Action Man today. Danced with joy round Mum in the kitchen, singing *Just Mum and me, Just Mum and me, No Action Man, Whoopee! Whoopee!* Mum gave a HUGE sigh and moaned, *Give it a rest, Finch – please!*

Tuesday, 13th July

Something weird happened at school today. I found myself feeling sorry for Shane Ripley. At breaktime there were some Year 3 kids calling him names and shouting stuff like *Shane-no brain!* And, *What's six times eight then, Shane?* And how he's only on Book 2 in maths, the same as them. They wouldn't leave him alone. So he roared after them, then along came Mr Buckeridge and hauled him off for bullying. I know Shane's a pain sometimes, but for a moment I saw this look on his face that made me feel for him. Those Year 3 kids may look sweet but some of them are little hooligans and are always winding him up. I will try to be more understanding and kinder to him in future, though there's no excuse for violence.

Looked up Kellogg in our telephone directory.

Not a single one. The only Kellogg I've heard of is the one who makes cornflakes. Those Kelloggs must be very rich. Maybe I'm a cornflake heiress and don't know it!

Action Man took Mum to the pub so I went up to Nolly's and we watched telly and played rummy. She wouldn't let me in till I promised not to nag her about smoking or go round checking her bins. That's all the thanks I get.

Our class's *Getting to Know You Visit* to Fletchley High tomorrow. Cassie's really mopy that she's not coming. It's bad enough that she's getting something I'd do anything for – but to hear her moan about it all the time...grrrrrr!

Wish 16.

I wish that I get to sit next to someone nice and certainly no boys. They are too immature at this age.

Wish 17.

I wish I don't get the most boring pathetic teachers. If I don't get to St Mon's then I want the best of the rest.

Wednesday, 14th July

Getting to Know You Day at Fletchley High
I got to know...

1. Jay! **SWOON! SWOON!** More about
that later.
2. Fletchley High School stinks. Well the
school hall does – of fish fingers. And the
cloakrooms smell of old socks.
3. The roof leaks. There were buckets down
the corridors catching the drips.
4. I am the second tallest in the class.
5. There are lots of midget immature boys.
6. There is a severe shortage of green acres,
lakes, woods and ponies. Just concrete, a fish
tank in the entrance hall and a horrid hairy
spider in the girls' loo.
7. SHANE RIPLEY IS NOT IN MY CLASS!
Wish no. 8 granted! Wishes do come true!
Miracles DO happen!
8. I am in the top sets for everything.
9. Our tutor group is 8MA.
10. Our year group tutor is Mr Anthony
Morris. He teaches Art and we are based
in one of the art rooms. He seems OK. But
he should get rid of the beard and learn
some new jokes.

11. There are 34 kids in our group. Cassie's will be twelve!

12. There was a total show-off with a mobile phone in his blazer. A real phoney! Ha ha!

It all looked so brilliant when Mum and I visited the open evening but now I know about St Mon's it seems crummy somehow.

BUT NOW...FOR THE MOST FANTASTIC AMAZING NEWS!

When we arrived there were loads of kids from other schools. Kayleigh and Carmen were giving marks out of ten for some of the boys. I was trying to keep away. Some of those boys barely reach my knees – they're the sort who make corny jokes about telegraph poles and roll around laughing about it.

THEN...KERPOW! I noticed this boy walking in through the gate. He was tall with brown hair. He looked really cool and laid back, not showing off like some – a Year 9 boy, at least. There was something really special about him, the way he walked with his head down, deep in thought. Then it started to rain and we all filed into the hall. And he came too!

He IS in my year! NOT ONLY THAT, but in

MY tutor group. NOT ONLY THAT, but on
MY table! (With Kayleigh and a boy called
Dan.) NOT ONLY THAT,
but his name is Jay!
Get it? Finch and Jay!
Bird buddies! I bet it
won't be long before the
tweet-tweet jokes start,
but I don't care a hoot!
(Joke) Actually, his name
badge said Jacob but he
borrowed my Tippex and
changed it to JAY. When he gave it back his
hand touched mine — and my tummy went
BOYNG-BOYNG-BOYNG!

We are in the same sets for Maths, English,
French and Science. He is the tallest in the
class and I'm the second. I can't stop thinking
about him. This is stupid. I don't have time
for boys. My hormones are going crazy! I
have put my Tippex on my shelf of treasures.

I phoned Cassie as soon as I could and told
her about Jay. I thought we'd got cut off
because when I'd finished there was total
silence. I said, *Cassie? Are you there?* She
grunted, *Yeah,* in a very moody way.

So I said, *What's the matter, Cass?*

Off she went − I thought you didn't like boys! Anyway, why should I be interested in Fletchley School when I'm not going there? Are you deliberately trying to make me feel worse?

If I hadn't been in such a good mood I'd have put the phone down. Instead I said, *Look Cassie − if I had a choice, Fletchley and Jay or you and St Mon's − there'd be no contest. Jay and Fletchley would win hands down!*

She screamed, *What!* So I said, *Only joking, Cass. But I might easily change my mind if you don't stop being such a pain! You're not the only one with problems!*

Cancel the second part of **Wish** 16! I definitely DO want to sit next to a boy − if he's Jay!

Thursday, 15th July

Cassie was very low today. She had ate a Mars bar *and* a Snickers at break. She says she needs regular doses of chocolate to keep her sane.

8.10. The Action Man arrived this evening loaded with shopping and announced that he was going to treat us to one of his special stir-fries. Not, *Would you **like** me to cook one of my special stir-fries?* I told him not to bother for me as I didn't like the look of those weird mushrooms he'd bought. I said, *I'm not eating those. They look like old men's ears.*

We don't get to choose anything any more. He hates telly except for football and sport. Mum and me **hate** football and sport and **love** telly. Now he's telling us what to eat. His mobile phone kept going off too. He is using our house like his office. I told him I saw a programme on telly that said mobiles can cook your brains like a microwave. He said his grandad used to cook sheeps' brains and have them on toast. I feel totally sick now.

Mum said she can't make it to Sports Day tomorrow. Faked big disappointment. She always used to win the mothers' race, which was brilliant when I was in the Infants but now it's just embarrassing especially as I am useless at sport.

8.45 p.m. Have just discovered my dirty PE kit still in the laundry basket. Got really mad at Mum. I could not believe it when the Action Man said, *No problem. Throw them over, I'll do them. It'll only take a jiffy.* As if I want his paws on my stuff!

I shut myself in my room but Mum followed me in sheepishly, saying it had just slipped her mind. I told her I understood *perfectly* how that could happen, seeing as she was too busy curled up on the settee watching telly with her boyfriend to remember about her one and only daughter's Sports Day which she couldn't be bothered to come to anyway. Mum looked a bit guilty then, so I felt a bit mean – for about one **millisecond** – but delighted that she'd got the message. I could see myself in my wardrobe mirror, looking totally miserable Then, as a joke, Mum pulled her mouth down like a sad clown – which made me mad again.

It's not a joke – and it's not funny! I screamed.

She said, *Look, Finch, it's not Ian's fault, you know. It's mine. He's trying really hard to be friends with you. Just give him a chance, will you!*

That did it. I wanted to scream, *ME! Give HIM a chance! Have you given ME a chance!*

A chance to say what I think! About how everything's changed since he marched in and started taking over! We were all right before he came. And do you know what's it's like seeing you all lovey-dovey! Only I'm not allowed to say what I think because you want be to be nice to him and I'm fed up with trying to be nice! I HATE HIM! I LOATHE HIM AND DESPISE HIM! Only you won't give me the chance to say it! But all that came out was a feeble, I hate him!

She gave a big sigh and snapped, Well, you've made that perfectly clear, haven't you!

Then she went all weepy, telling me how much it matters that I like him.

I don't know what I'd do without Graeme. He is next to me on my pillow. His fur is all wet from my tears. My tummy is rumbling with hunger.

Friday, 16th July

7.55. My eyes look terrible this morning, all red and puffy. I pointed them out to Mum. My PE kit is still damp. Please let it rain and Sports Day be cancelled.

5.15. THE WORST SPORTS DAY IN MY ENTIRE LIFE.

Shane came second in the 50 metres so, trying to be encouraging, I went up to him and said, *Well done, Shane. That was brilliant.* Then it was the stupid obstacle race. I managed to skip to the stupid bench and crawl under, hop to the stupid bucket, fill the stupid bucket with water using a stupid paper cup, when I heard, *Come on Finch! You can do it!*

I looked round, and saw Mum and Action Man waving and yelling at me. That's when I flipped — then tripped. The bucket went flying, I got a soaking and everyone found it hilarious. It was all over by the time I'd picked myself up. I didn't even look at Mum as I squelched into school to change. Is there no escape from the Action Man? Then Cassie, Carmen and Kayleigh came running up to say that Shane's been telling everyone I fancy him! AAAAARGH!!!

Yes-Mum-it-was-a-brilliant-idea-of-Mr-Tanner's-to-surprise-me-by-turning-up-

at-Sports-Day-and-I-am-truly-grateful-that-you-managed-to-get-an-hour-off-work-and-Mr-Tanner-went-to-all-the-trouble-to-give-you-a-lift-and-come along-to-cheer-me on, I said to Mum in my robot voice, when she got home from work and had a go at me for being sulky and ungrateful. She said, *Finch, this isn't like you.* I used my robot voice again. *Who-is-it-like-then?* Then I did my robot walk to my room and slammed the door. If I'm treated like a robot with no feelings then I might as well act like one.

It's the last time I try to be understanding about Shane Ripley. Or about Mum and the Action Man.

Saturday, 17th July
My chest has grown **2.7 cms!** My hormones are definitely on the move. I might need a bra soon.

I went to the library this morning and asked how I could trace people by the name of Kellogg. I discovered:

1. Two American brothers, John and Will Kellogg, invented the cornflake in 1898.
2. There aren't many people called Kellogg.

I know this because the librarian said I should try all the other telephone directories.
I counted **149** of them for the British Isles!
I searched eleven of them – not a single Kellogg so far.

Met up with Cassie in town. We were both feeling fed up so we played **The Next Person Who...** to take our minds off things. I pointed to the bench opposite the ice-cream kiosk and said to her, *The next person who...sits on that bench is your boyfriend.*
There was this fat, bald, tattooed bloke in a vest and shorts, eating chips and walking towards it. Cassie was jumping up and down, screaming, *No, help!*

PER-LEEEZ! Don't sit down! Don't! Don't! I can't bear it! But he plonked himself down right there, and Cassie was shrieking and groaning and laughing at the same time. I got a stitch from laughing. People were staring at us. We felt a lot better after that. I'm pretty good at inventing games and cheering people up.

Surprise, surprise. Action Man was here when I got home, painting the windows he bashed to bits getting open. When Mum popped out to get some milk I asked him if Mum had told him about my dad. He said, *Yeah, she did,* looking pathetically surprised and grateful that I was speaking to him, which I usually avoid if I can.

So I said, *Well, you'll understand, then. No one could ever replace him. Never. She's had boyfriends before, you know. Some of them were really nice.* (Her only boyfriend was the horrible Ray Beasley actually.) *But none of them lasted. Because deep deep down, Mum's still madly in love with my dad and no one can ever match up to him. So, don't be too disappointed when it happens to you. Because no one could ever take his place. Not ever. But don't worry about it. We're fine as we are. We don't need anyone else.*

He just stared at me. He didn't say a word. One up to me, I think. Graeme and me went to my room, put on some loud music and danced and laughed. Hee-hee-hee.

Mum got two numbers on the lottery, I got one. I played our Lottery Fantasy Game inside my head with me pushing the Action Man over the side of our yacht and watching the black fins of sharks moving in and then the waters churning and thrashing. Mum said, *What are you smiling about, Finch?*

mmm Ian flavour....

Sunday, 18th July

Mum's bought some trainers and taken up jogging with the A. Man. She told me they only cost £20 but I found the price tag which said **£65!** I thought we were supposed to be broke. Nolly's gone on a coach outing to Windsor Castle. I am becoming a neglected child.

Went roller-blading with Cassie, Carmen and Kayleigh. I'm getting pretty good and can go backwards now. Cassie was a bit moody about being left out as we were nattering about Fletchley. We think we might go for skirts after all and not trousers. Not that I have given up on St Mon's yet.

I went back to Cassie's after. Everyone was out. She showed me all this slinky lingerie her mum has bought herself for their holiday – it must have cost a fortune. We tried some of it on. Cassie put on this long, clingy, gold, silky number with a plunging front. She looked about twenty-two!

7.30. Started on a design for my bedroom makeover. I want it hi-tech, all sleek and organised. No more frilly stuff and pastel colours but something really **KERPOW!** Red, deep blue, silver and gold. I showed it to Mum. She said, *Fat chance, Finch.*

I'm going to make some storage from cardboard boxes and paint them silver or use kitchen foil. It will keep me busy during the holidays. I'm fed up with being poor. We can't even afford a holiday. Cassie's going to Florida in two weeks. She gets all the luck.

Monday, 19th July

There was an infantile note going round the

class today with a drawing – supposed to be
ME – me kissing Shane! And saying, *Shane,
Shane, I LUV YOU!* My own stupid fault for
trying to be kind and understanding. I only
had to turn round and see the grinning faces
of certain boys to know who was responsible.
At breaktime, those same pathetic saddos,
namely, Lenny, Neil and Shane, found it
amusing to follow us around calling, *Here he
is! Your boyfriend. Don't you want to snog
him then?* And Shane licking his lips and
making kissy slurping noises.

So I said, *All right! Come on then!*

Then me, Cassie, Kayleigh and Carmen got
them to follow us to the pig swill bins behind
the kitchen. Then we pounced! But we only
managed to grab Neil, so Cassie and Carmen
sat on him, saying, *No, it's Neil we all love!
We just can't resist that big spot on
your nose! And those skinny legs
and your flapping ears!*
We held him
hostage all
breaktime.
Poor thing
– he could
hardly breathe.

we love neil
heee hee

Shane and Lenny got bored after a while and wandered off. Shane looked quite disappointed. Honestly, they are *so* sad.

I know Jay would not do anything so pathetically immature.

Tuesday, 20th July

Nine Things I Hate about the Action Man

1. His eyes constantly swivelling at Mum.
2. His embarrassing impressions of Sean Connery for Nolly and calling her Mish Moneypenny, like he's James Bond.
3. His pongy trainers on the mat.
4. The loo after he's been in it! Phew! And the way he always leaves the seat up and uses OUR shower and towels on his horrible, sweaty, hairy body after he's been jogging.
5. His obsession with fixing things. Mum and me LIKED the bathroom door not shutting properly. We could have cosy chats. There was no need to lock doors before HE came! We never had secrets till now!
6. Always saying, *It'll only take a jiffy!*
7. The way he craftily gets Mum away from me, e.g. taking her jogging.
8. His rude comments on what we like to

eat, e.g. listing out loud the ingredients of
the Mr Whippy Cream Dessert that Mum was
whisking up and saying, *Have you read this?
It's nothing but chemicals.*

9. The way he tries to suck up to me, like
giving me those hair clips and an Alice band
that I really wanted. As if I didn't know that
Mum put him up to it. So I told him they
were the wrong sort. I refuse to wear them.

I could go on but I don't want to think about
him any more. It is too depressing.

   I put Dad's photo on top of the telly before
I came to bed. He'll be looking straight at
them as they snuggle up on the settee. I hope
Mum feels guilty.

Wednesday, 21st July

No proper lessons today, just taking stuff down
from the walls, tearing out the clean pages
from our books so we can take the tatty
remains home. Shane tore all his work up. Miss
Phipps got cross and sent him out into the
corridor where he rearranged the drawing pins
on the pinboard to spell **BUM**

Sam Leishman kidded him it should have a
silent B like in thumb so now it says

I can't believe tomorrow is the last day
ever at this school.

Called in at the library and waded through
fifteen more telephone directories. Still no
Kelloggs. Twenty-six down, only 123 to go. I
asked Mum where Dad came from so I could
narrow it down a bit. She sighed, *Look Finch,
it's a long time ago. Please don't dig it up
again.* I told her that even if she could forget
Dad so easily I could not. She clasped her
hands to her head and let out a long groan.

Thursday, 22nd July
LAST DAY EVER AT PERCY ALLSOP
COMBINED SCHOOL!

I gave Miss Phipps a drawing I did of
Graeme, and some flowers from the garden.
She had loads of prezzies. Finished tidying the
classroom. Played board games. Watched
Teachers versus Year 7 rounders match. All
the staff dressed up as usual. Mr Buckeridge

was Superman again. Same old ladder in his tights as last year. Had very last Assembly and sang *'I'd like to teach, the world to sing'*, followed by *'One more step along the world I go'*. Tears were running down my face. Loads of us were crying. Even Shane looked a bit lost. Like Mr Buckeridge said, this is the end of one of life's journeys and the beginning of another. Back in the classroom Shane yelled, *Three cheers for Miss Phipps!* She went all stunned and weepy.

B U M B is still on the pinboard.

Goodbye, school! Goodbye, desk! Goodbye, Miss Phipps! **SOB! SOB!** What does the future hold, I wonder? Especially for Cassie all alone at St Monica's and me at Fletchley without Cassie. For nine years we have shared playgroup and schooldays and everything is changing. We were blubbing non-stop. I had to keep getting paper from the toilets for us.

I keep thinking about Jay. Graeme is dying to meet him. Graeme is the only person I get any sympathy from these days.

Friday, 23rd July

First day of the holidays. Feels weird because nothing's the same any more.

I asked Nolly if she'd made her doctor's appointment yet. She nearly bit my head off. She is not a jolly Nolly and needs all the encouragement she can get. So, when she wasn't looking Graeme and I found her ciggies and wrote some helpful messages on them with my felt-tips, like,

WHY DON'T YOU HAVE A MINT HUMBUG
INSTEAD? 20 A DAY = **£1,000** A YEAR.

Just got back from Cassie's. All she wanted to do was show off her holiday clothes. I got fed up with her making faces at everything *I* suggested doing. I wasn't feeling exactly bouncy myself. Then her mum came in and said, *What's the matter with you two?* And Cassie said, *Finch is in a bad mood because her mum's got a boyfriend.* As if it was me being a pain! Anyway, I don't want people thinking that the Action Man is anything to do with Mum, especially Cassie's mum because she's a right gossip. So I said, *He's not a boyfriend. He just does a few odd jobs around the house.* And Cassie's mum said, *Sounds like a man in a million. Send him round here!*

Cassie got even grumpier so I came home.

Mum just announced the exciting plans for the weekend. A 'taster' day at the Heron Canoe Centre with barbecue, games and competitions. **I DO NOT THINK SO!** No way am I being seen in public with the Hairy One, making a fool of myself. So I said, very sorry I couldn't go because Cassie had invited me for the weekend.

Had to phone her and grovel SOR-REEE and beg to stay. I think it's child cruelty when you can't even stay in your own house without being forced into doing things you loathe with people you loathe. He is getting right up my nostrils!

Haven't even got enough money for a lottery ticket!

Goodbye, dear notebook. I'm off to Cassie's. I'm not risking Leo the Pest snooping in my bag and finding you. I don't want Cassie peeking either. So see you soon!

Sunday, 25th July

I AM SO ANGRY! It's A COMPLETE
INVASION! How DARE he come into my room!
How could Mum let him! I cannot believe it!

I might have guessed something was up
when I got back this evening. The way they
were looking so pleased with themselves,
watching me as I opened my bedroom door.
Then I saw why. I saw pots of
paint and red and blue walls,
shelves painted silver, a blue
ceiling with gold stars, even
my bed painted gold. Exactly
like the design I'd drawn. I
couldn't speak. All I could
think was that HE had invaded
my room. And Mum had let him. My private
personal space. THE ONLY SPACE I'VE GOT
OF MY OWN!!! And how I'd loved my design
and been looking forward to doing it myself.
And now it's completely ruined – because
he's barged in and taken over again. I could
smell his sweaty smell all over my room.
I **HATE** it now.

Mum was smiling and the Action Man was

leaning against the door, looking smug. All my books and private things were piled on the floor. And balancing on the top was my *Blue Peter* jigsaw with this notebook and all my secret stuff inside. I rushed over to grab it. And that's when I noticed the new leg on my bed, where there used to be a pile of old books propping it up. I heard myself screaming, *What have you done with my pile of books? I liked the books! They were more interesting! I don't want a boring old wooden leg!* Who said you could come into my room! I wanted to rip the leg off and hit him over his stupid grinning head with it.

Then Nolly bustled in, rattling on about how Mum and him had been up half the night to get it finished in time. And how she'd painted the shelves and the bed, showing me the paint on her fingers. I felt bad about that. It wasn't Nolly's fault. I wanted to say something but I couldn't. I threw myself on to my bed and started crying. It was like I'd been holding it all in and once I started I couldn't stop. I had my face buried in the pillow but I heard Nolly say, *Och, dinna take on. She's at tha' difficult age. Let her be for a wee while.*

Then I heard the back door bang and it went quiet. I was checking that my notebook was safe when Mum came charging back. *How could you be so revolting! You could at least have said thank you! We thought it'd be a lovely surprise. How could you do that? You've really hurt his feelings, you know!*

So I yelled back at her, *Oh, poor thing! What about MY feelings? How would YOU like it if I brought MY friends into YOUR room and went through YOUR personal things! How could you let him in my room, mauling my stuff!*

She ranted on and on. *Why, Finch? Why are you behaving like this? He's been so good to you! What's he done to make you hate him so much?*

Everything! I screamed. *Everything about him! The way he practically lives here! The space he takes up! His smell! He's taking over! I just don't understand how YOU can like him!*

Well I DO! I like him very very much!

So I said, *Yeah? Well, you liked Ray Beasley too, didn't you! Only you were wrong about HIM, weren't you? What if he's like him?*

He isn't! she glared. *He's nothing like him!*

And why can't you ever call Ian by his name?

His name is Mr Tanner, isn't it?

Would it really hurt to call him, Ian? Would it?

YES! IT RUDDY WELL WOULD!

I stood hugging my jigsaw box while she carried on about all the trouble he'd gone to getting someone to cover for him at the Canoe Centre so he could do my room as a surprise for when I got back.

I didn't ruddy well ask him to, did I? I screamed.

I stared down at my *Blue Peter* jigsaw box, my tears dripping on to its lid. Mum barked, *Look at me, Finch! Not that stupid jigsaw!*

It's not stupid! It reminds me of when it was just you and me, and we did things together!

That's what you want, is it? she snorted. *Just you and me, growing into two little old ladies, doing everything together for ever and ever! What happens when you get a boyfriend? Because I expect you will, one day. Shall I go all sulky and insist you stay in so we can do jigsaws together? Shall I make faces and do ape impressions behind their back, like you do? Shall I yawn when they* talk? Shall I groan when they arrive? Shall I hold my nose and spray air freshener everywhere every time they use the bathroom? Shall I shrug and mutter DUNNO whenever they ask a question? Honestly, Finch, I don't know how he's put up with you! You've always been so grown up, you know, so sensible. But lately you've been behaving like a brat!

I rushed out to find poor Graeme. He'd been locked up in his hutch most of the weekend. He says he'd be mighty mad too if some bossy rabbit moved in and rearranged his hutch. As I told him all about it, it got me thinking. Maybe I've been going about things the wrong way. Telling Mum how I really feel has only made her stick up for the Action Man and get angry with me. It should be the other way round! Mum ought to be on my side, oughtn't she? So, I've got a new plan. I'm going to do things differently. I'm going to be just as smarmy as the Action Man. From now on I'm going to be sickeningly nice and helpful. That way Mum can't blame *me* for being difficult. But I'll make sure she sees how he's slowly coming between us and taking over.

I've started by apologising. OK Mum. I'm

sorry if I was rude. I know he means a lot to you. I'll do my best not to let you down again. I hope you're right about him because I don't want you getting hurt, OK?

I was Little Miss Perfect. Now she's all cuddles and, *I know it can't be easy for you, love. I do understand, really.* But she doesn't.

I can't stop crying. My face looks like mashed potato. I hate him more than ever. I hate her for liking him. We were happy before he came. He's spoilt everything. I'm not going to call him Ian though. I won't call him anything.

Disgusting bristly black hairs stuck in the bath plughole – makes me feel sick. Ages ago I heard someone on the telly say *incandescent with rage.* I looked *incandescent* up. It means giving a bright light when heated up. I've been saving it up for some place to use it and now I can. I AM INCANDESCENT WITH RAGE.

Mum's going to be so sorry she didn't listen to me.

JUST WAIT AND SEE!

Monday, 26th July

Had an excellent dream where the A. Man fell off his ladder into a passing refuse lorry and got minced into small pieces. No sign of him today except hairs in plughole. Mum asked if it would help if he didn't come round so much. Felt like jumping up and down with delight — till she added that we could go to his place instead because he's got a little house in Trinity Street opposite the church. I wanted to yell, *No way!*

Then I remembered my new plan so I said, in my sweetest angelic voice, *No, it's all right, Mum. I suppose it's only fair to you that he comes here sometimes. But just remind him he doesn't own the place, right?*

But I was thinking, You've got to be **joking.** That's enemy territory. I'm not going to be seen dead there. And how come she knows so much about his house? Is that where she goes when she tells me she's been doing overtime?

I've put some of my things back on the shelves but only to hide my notebook. Can't really be bothered. They can stay on the floor for all I care. They will be my silent protest against the invader.

I just found this letter on my pillow. Graeme is truly the world's kindest and cleverest bunny. I'm sticking it in.

---

dear finch
just to let yoo no yoo can deepend on me
you did not no i cood rite did yoo
well i can
i hav lernt a lot from sitting on yor desk
wen yoo rite yor book
i like the pikcha you did of me in a skool blaza
cood yoo do won of me on rolla blayds pleez
cheer up it mayks me sad wen yor sad
pleezs cood you not slobba on me so much
as my fur is getting slymee
can we play sniff and dig soon
eny charns of sum mor grayps

lots of luv yor best bunny graeme

Dear Graeme
Thank you for your lovely
letter. You are the one
true friend that I can
always trust. You deserve
all the grapes you want.
Here is a picture of you in
your rollerblades.

One whole day without the A. Man!
A miracle!

Tuesday, 27th July
Have moved this notebook and other secret
things into my old Buckaroo box.

11.07. Bored. Bored. ~~Bored~~. Shall I ring
Cassie? Graeme says Nope. Not after all he's
heard about how she was a pain all weekend.
Mope, mope about St Mon's. Drool, drool
about Leah's brother. Nearly having a nervous
breakdown because she's got two spots;
weighing herself, groaning, then scoffing two
KitKats. But if I mention the Action Man, she
whines, *Oh not that again! It's not as bad as
my parents who row all the time.*
　　She's getting really fat.

1.35. Just got back from the library. Thirteen more telephone directories but still no Kelloggs. Where are they?

Had a brilliant idea at the library – need Dad's photo first.

2.50. Took Dad's photo to the library and used the photocopier to enlarge it. It is **AMAZING.** Have now got three poster-sized Dads smiling at me from my bedroom door, the kitchen wall and over the mirror in the bathroom! How ya doing, Dad?

Another day free of the A. Man. **Hurrah!** Mum working late today. Graeme and I will cook her something nice. No, not grapes, Graeme. It's just like the old days. I think Mum is feeling a little bit guilty now because she bought me some fruit-flavoured lip balms and a magazine. She looked quite stunned by my posters.

My horoscope says: 'Someone is driving you up the wall this week, but you know what to do, don't you?' I certainly do. Also, 'Pink is your lucky colour – you could make a big impression on someone.' Changed into my pink T-shirt. I'm feeling much better.

I have written a new tune for my recorder. I am astounded by my talents!

Mum keeps looking at my posters. I thought she was going to say something but she didn't. She was a bit quiet to tell the truth. Maybe she's starting to realise that she could never love anyone like she loved my dad. Especially the you-know-who.

Wednesday, 28th July

I knew it was too good to last. The A. Man has been here all evening. I played my new recorder tune to Mum and the A. Man. It starts all happy and lovey-dovey, builds up to a great crashing noise, then there's a pause, followed by lots of slow, sad, wailing sounds.

I could see the Action Man stifling a yawn but he gave a little clap when I'd finished. Mum smiled proudly. I *accidentally* left the music sheet on top of the coffee table in front of the A. Man while Mum was upstairs. I saw him glance at it then pick it up and read the title, *In Memory of my Dead Father*. He glared, *Don't you think you ought to put this somewhere safe?* I snatched it off him and put it in my music folder. When Mum came back I asked him very sweetly if he'd like a cup of coffee. Does he know he has a pimple on his neck?

Thursday, 29th July

So bored I phoned Cassie. She says she's going to a friend's house! What friend? I'm the only friend she's got. She says she met a girl when her mum took her to Henley's for her St Mon's uniform. She's a new girl too and their mums got chatting. She lives only a couple of streets away and they'll be catching the school pick-up coach together. The girl is really nice and friendly. *Oh, how truly delightful for you*, I said in a posh voice. *I'm sure you'll have a simply wonderful time together! Be careful you don't squash her pony when you sit on it!*

Cassie said, *You're just jealous!* and
slammed the phone down. Phoned Kayleigh.
She was out. Phoned Carmen. Her mum's
taking her shopping for holiday clothes.
Phoned Leah. No answer. Didn't feel like doing
anything. Just moped about.

Mum's just come home from work and says
that one of the A. Man's friends has invited
them to a party on Saturday. She blabbered
on about how she's so excited because she
hasn't been to a dress-up party for years, and
Carol's going to lend her a dress, and faffing
about what shoes to wear and she might treat
herself to some new earrings and I can help
her choose.

I don't know how I managed it, but I kept
to my plan. I pretended to be pleased and
interested in the stupid party. I chatted
about hairstyles and earrings and stuff. Then I
came in here and slobbered all over Graeme.

Why is all this happening to me?

The A. Man was here this evening so Graeme
and me went up to Nolly's. She said I looked
like a week of wet Sundays, so made me some

of her Nolly's Magic Medicine, which is a banana and chocolate milk shake. When I was little it was Nolly's Super-duper Prize for Being a Good Little Girl.

While she was in the kitchen we had a peep in the Little Miss Neat money box I lent her. There was only 57p in it. There should have been a lot more than that if she's really cut down on her smoking. Graeme said it was time for action so we hid her ciggies behind the Virgin Mary.

She couldn't watch more than ten minutes of *Eastenders* before she was panting for a smoke and started looking around for ciggies. We pretended we didn't notice. Then she snapped, *Right, Missie! What have ye done with them? Hand them over!*

We acted all innocent but she threatened we'd be banned from visiting if we didn't give them back — so we did. She lit up, took a big drag, and said, *Have ye no' got anything better to do, lass, than wear a poor old woman's nerves to pieces?*

So I said, well, I could do with a ciggie then — my nerves were suffering too. I grabbed Nolly's and took a drag. Then I started coughing and felt like puking. She

went mad and ended up chasing me round the room. I told her it was her own fault – all that passive smoking I'd been doing for years had got to me at last. Why does anyone smoke? **UGH!**

Nolly had to sit down to get her breath back after that. Then she started laughing. But that made her cough and then she got a pain in her chest. She didn't look at all well so I made her a cup of tea. I told her that if the A. Man doesn't take a hike I might have to move in with her. She threw up her hands and said, *Lord, help me!* I think she was only joking.

Friday, 30th July

Cassie goes on holiday to Florida today. She hasn't even phoned me!

Went round to Kayleigh's with Carmen. Kayleigh shares a room with her big sister but she was at work so we tried on some of her clothes. I kept my vest on. Carmen was wearing a bra. She's only had it two days. She was really showing off in it. She's going on holiday to Spain tomorrow. I've only been on a school day trip to Calais.

Mum's started wearing all this sporty gear, vests and jogging pants. I don't know where the money's coming from. Not only do I have to put up with this fitness stuff but she's become a health freak too. I do not like salad with wheatgerm and raw beansprouts! I told her that Graeme is the rabbit, not me. We know whose fault this is, don't we Graeme?

The A. Man here as usual. Gave him big welcome smile and made him a cup of coffee, but spat in it when he wasn't looking. Gave even bigger smile when he drank it.

Mum says Kayleigh can stay over tomorrow night to keep me company while they're at the party, but I'm not to nag Nolly about smoking as it's making her ill.

Mum's been trying on some of Carol's posh dresses. I chose the black one. I'm not having her wearing the red one, it showed too much chest. I'm being so nice and understanding I'm beginning to make myself feel sick.

I think my plan is beginning to work. I've been putting on a kind and helpful, but at the same time, a sad, lonely expression, and sighing a lot. I don't say much. Just nod or shake my head or shrug, *I don't mind.* I'm sure she's feeling a bit guilty now about letting the A. Man cause all this grief. She bought me a box of glitter nail varnishes and

keeps fussing over me. But I'm not going to be bought off. I've got to think of ways to get her more on my side. **HE HAS TO GO!**

Saturday, 31st July
Mum's on two weeks' holiday from today.

Things I'd Like to Do this Holiday

1. Visit Alton Towers and go on the Corkscrew, Oblivion and the Congo River Rapids.
2. Go shopping for some new clothes – NOT school uniform. Why do all the shops have big signs saying BACK TO SCHOOL? We don't want to be reminded about school. It's the holidays for flipping sakes!
3. Take Nolly to Swanage.
4. Make a fitness track for Graeme.

I will copy this list and stick it on the kitchen wall.

5. Carry on being nice (but looking miserable and left out – which I am!), so Mum feels really guilty about neglecting me and siding with the A. Man. If she really loves me she will get rid of him. He is only a visitor – not part of our family.

I will not stick this on the kitchen wall.

7.45. Took Mum breakfast in bed. She moaned and groaned when I opened the curtains. I told her mornings are the best part of the day when everything is new and fresh. I get all my best thinking done first thing in the morning.

9.45. Tidied up and polished while Mum and the A. Man were out jogging.
   Picked some flowers from Nolly's garden and made the flat look nice.

13.00. Cooked a pizza and chips from the freezer.

14.15. Invited myself along when they went shopping and chatted to Action Man all the way home about canoeing like I was really interested.

17.30. Made them sit down in the sitting

room and took them coffee and biscuits while
I made tea. It was pretty amazing if I do say
so myself. I made a face with some mashed
potato, with boiled eggs cut in half for eyes,
a tomato for a nose and a sausage for a
smiling mouth and some grated cheese for
hair. I've put a real hair in the A. Man's.

Heard the A. Man say to Mum (I had my
ear pressed to the sitting-room door):

A. MAN: *What's she playing at, Debs?*
MUM: *What d'you mean?*
A. MAN: *Well, it's not normal is it?*
           Why isn't she out with her
           friends? Why is she suddenly
           going overboard to be so nice
           to me?
MUM: (Sharpish) *Of course it's normal!*
           She's always been helpful — and
           she's trying really hard to make
           up for last week. How can you
           say that!

              LONG PAUSE

A. MAN: *You know what I think? I think*
           maybe she's trying to make you
           feel a bit guilty too. (He is
           not as stupid as I thought.)

MUM: *What? Look, please don't try and tell me about my own daughter. It's just her way of saying sorry for last weekend. I told you she apologised, but it's not easy for her to say it to you. She's trying so hard, you know! Let me decide what is and isn't normal, thank you very much!* (Yeah!)

A. MAN: *She doesn't look too happy though, does she?*

PAUSE

Look, Debs – why don't we give this party a miss and stay in? (What's he playing at? Is he trying to get round me? So he can act like he's my best friend or something?)
We can have an evening of passion! Grrr! (YEEE-UCK! Excuse me while I puke!)

MUM: (Giggling) *Don't be daft! Look – she says she doesn't mind. And Nolly's here. Anyway – I've been*

really looking forward to this
party and dressing up. (I *do* mind!)
Then, after tea they had a brilliant squabble.
Mum was getting ready and the A. Man
started running the water for the washing-up.
It makes me mad every time I see him acting
like he's at home here. So I said, *No! Leave it
to me. You go and get ready for the party.
Off you go and enjoy yourselves. I'll be all
right, I'll have Graeme, Nolly and Kayleigh to
keep me company.*

I got a bit carried away actually, like I
was Cinderella or something. We had a sort
of tug of war over the washing-up-liquid
bottle, with me shouting, *No! I want to do it!
Really!*

Mum came back in then. She was all made
up, wearing her sexy black dress and silver
earrings and necklace, and she looked beautiful.
And I saw the A. Man's eyes swivelling all over
her, and I wanted to hit him with the
saucepan. She saw the look on my face – I was
trying not to cry. So Mum started pushing him
out, saying, *It's all
right, Ian. She* likes *doing it. Go and get ready.*

About time! I thought, *Mum's taking my side.*

But would he listen? No. *She's just a kid — she shouldn't be doing all this,* he said.

Mum caught my eye then. **See?** I beamed a thought message to her. **I told you he was taking over.**

Look, Ian, she said firmly, *let Finch do things her own way.*

But still he went on. *I can't just stand here watching. Shove over, Finch. You can go and watch telly if you want.* And he started scrubbing at the plates.

So I shoved him back, saying, *I don't mind! Honestly!* He sighed and picked up the tea towel.

I prefer to let them drain actually, I told him. *It's more hygienic.*

Then Mum snapped, *Ian! just leave it, will you? Please! We're going to be late if we don't get a move on. Finch will see to it, won't you love? You don't mind, do you?*

I wanted to yell, YEAH! I DO! I do mind! I wanted her to stay and him to go. I wanted things to be like they were before. But instead I attacked the saucepan with a knife, noisily scraping off all the burnt bits, blinking like mad to stop the tears.

He grabbed another tea towel and tossed it

to Mum. *Come on*, he grinned. *It won't take a jiffy. We're not leaving till it's done. There are laws against child labour, you know.*

That did it. I think it was meant to be a joke, but Mum didn't get it. He was acting just like that social worker when I was little and Mum wasn't well, asking questions and checking up on whether I was being neglected. She glared at him. *I don't MAKE her do it!*

Yeah, I know. All I'm saying is...

What! barked Mum.

Never mind, he said. Because Kayleigh arrived then.

I wanted to say to Mum, *Now you can see I'm right. He's bossing YOU now. Can't you see that's how it will always be if you don't tell him to get lost? And why are you going with **him**? And leaving **me** here!*

I stood at the door waving, just like Cinderella in her kitchen. I don't know how Mum could go off like that. HOW COULD SHE?

Got to go. Kayleigh wants to know what I'm writing. I feel like crying.

Sunday, 1st August
Something **REALLY REALLY BAD** happened

last night. Nolly was rushed into hospital. Nolly, me and Kayleigh were watching telly when Nolly's phone started ringing upstairs. Off she went to answer it but she was gone for ages. I shouted up the stairs but she didn't answer. When I went up I found her lying across her bed. I knew something was wrong. Her face was all white and wet-looking, she was breathing funny and she'd been a bit sick too and her lips had gone a funny blue colour. I called her name but she didn't answer. I yelled for Kayleigh then, but when she saw Nolly she started screaming because she thought she was dead.

All I could think of was that it might be a heart attack. And I remembered something I'd seen on telly, about what to do. So I yelled to Kayleigh, *Quick! Quick! We've got to find an aspirin! Look in the bathroom!*

I managed to get her sitting up a bit, and she started coming round a bit. So I said *It's all right, Nolly. It's all right.*

And I put the aspirin in her mouth and got her to chew it. Then I dialled 999 for an ambulance, and I phoned Mum on the Action Man's mobile. It seemed for ever till the ambulance arrived. Then everything happened so fast. The ambulance man and lady were so nice that I started crying then, because of the way they were rushing about with the oxygen mask and injections. I told them about the aspirin and they said I'd done exactly the right thing. Then they strapped Nolly into a chair and she disappeared into the ambulance, and it roared away with the siren going. I thought she was going to die.

Kayleigh had rung her mum. She came straight round and we followed the ambulance to the hospital, its siren was going all the way. A bit later Mum arrived with the A. Man.

I didn't see Nolly again because she'd gone into Intensive Care. She really has had a heart attack. We didn't get back home till 2.30 in the morning. The doctor said the aspirin would have helped her. But I keep thinking it must be my fault for taking Nolly's cigarettes and making her chase me round the room. Please God and Virgin Mary, please, please don't let Nolly die. I don't care about anything else. Cancel all my other wishes.

MY ONE AND ONLY Wish IS:
PLEASE, PLEASE MAKE NOLLY BETTER SOON.

I have said it 100 times.

Monday, 2nd August

I slept with Mum in her bed last night except we didn't get much sleep. Mum kept tossing and turning and blowing her nose and going on about how it was all her fault and she wished she'd never gone to the party. In the end we sat up and I had the idea of sending telepathic messages to Nolly to get better. The house seems so empty without her.

When we visited the hospital only Mum was allowed to see her so I had to wait with the A. Man. He tried putting his arm round me! I moved away and concentrated on more messages to Nolly. YOU WILL NOT DIE. **YOU ARE GETTING BETTER** – EVERY MINUTE YOU ARE GETTING BETTER AND BETTER. And I made pictures in my head of Nolly sitting up and smiling and asking for a cup of tea, and all the nurses and doctors looking amazed, saying, *It's a miracle!*

Mum was crying when she came back. She wouldn't tell me why at first but I nagged and nagged. The doctor told her that Nolly's still in danger — she could have another attack.

Mum took me shopping but we both felt so miserable we came home. Even the new jeans she bought me don't cheer me up.

Cassie likes Nolly. I wonder if she will send me a postcard.

Tuesday, 3rd August

I saw Nolly for a few minutes today. She was asleep but I held her hand so she'd know I was there. She is full of tubes and wired up to machines. They have taken out her false teeth. She looked so old and tiny, like she was shrinking. She looks bigger when she's bustling about.

Wednesday, 4th August

They are doing lots of tests on Nolly. They haven't said anything about cancer. This is the worst ever holiday in my life.

Graeme and me have made a card for Nolly. On the front is a picture of Mum, me and Graeme looking very sad and we're saying:

We're sad that you have been in pain
Get well and please come home again.
We love you lots, dearest Nolly
And when you're back...

Then inside, We'll all be jolly! And there's a picture of us smiling.

Thursday, 5th August

Nolly was trying to talk today. She kept mumbling about her teeth. We weren't allowed to stay too long in case it wears her out. Mum says we mustn't think about her having another attack, but think about her getting better and planning what to do when she gets home. She will need a lot of looking after. She must not climb stairs, so Mum's planning to swaps bedrooms with her but she doesn't know who will look after her when she's at work.

Went into town with Kayleigh. She wanted to play **The Next Person Who...** but it wasn't as funny as with Cassie and I didn't feel like laughing anyway.

I really miss Cassie. It's not the same with Kayleigh – I get bored after about ten minutes. What if Cassie doesn't want to be friends again?

Friday, 6th August

Nolly was in an ordinary ward today! She hasn't got so many wires and tubes now. We took some nighties in for her. The nurse was telling Nolly she must stop smoking for good as it puts her at greater risk of another attack!

Mum had to go and talk to the doctor. I was left with the Action Man. He was acting as if he was my friend, all chatty, telling me how Mum talked about me all the time. He said, *Go on – test me! Ask me what your first word was.* Mum had even told him about calling me her little alien from planet Neat! I nearly had a heart attack myself. How could she tell him all those secret things? He's the alien, not me. He's the one who doesn't belong. **The alien from the planet Creep.** I said, *Excuse me, I need the loo.*

☆   ☆   ☆

2.15. Kayleigh just phoned. They are having a barbecue and I can sleep over. Graeme is invited too. He'll sleep over with her little sister's guinea pig. I don't really want to go but Mum says it will do me good. Also the Action Man is coming today to move some of Mum's and Nolly's furniture round so I'm going because I can't stand any more of him. It's bad enough with having Nolly so ill without him poking his nose in. I have stuck a huge PRIVATE! KEEP OUT! speech balloon on my Dad poster on my door.

A TRUE STORY

Once upon a time there was a girl who lived happily with her mum and her gran. Then one day her mum got a boyfriend. The girl couldn't stand him but her mum was totally besotted with him. He pretended to like kids and sucked up to the girl.

Soon he was in their house nearly every day, acting as if he owned the place.

One day the girl came home to find he'd been in her bedroom and all her private things had been moved. He had this idea that if he decorated the girl's room for her she'd be thrilled and she'd have to like him and he'd have won. But the girl was furious – with him for invading her room – and with her mother for letting him!

Worse still, the mum took the man's side! The girl was in despair and angry with her mum for letting it happen. What she dreaded most of all was that the man would move in and completely take over.

A few days later, the girl came home from sleeping over at her friend's house after a barbecue party. She could tell straight away that the man had stayed the night in their flat. She was devastated and searched for her mum but she was out. The man was there though, in her mum's bedroom, moving some shelves. She saw his horrible hairy hands reach up and grab the presents the girl had made for her mum when she was little. The *Blue Peter* pencil pot and the little chest of drawers made from matchboxes, that had sat there unused for years, gathering dust. He tossed them on to the bed like rubbish. The girl was furious and told him to leave their things alone. She wanted to stop him touching any more of their things so she ran in and climbed the shelves to reach the other things. He shouted at her and tried to grab her.

She screamed, *You're not my dad! You can't tell me what to do! I hate you!* She couldn't hold it in any longer. She called him lots of names and tried pushing him out of the way.

That's when he lost his temper. He grabbed her and hit her – so hard she fell and caught her head on the shelves. There was blood running down her face.

He realised he'd made a big mistake then.

He started to grovel and say he was sorry, that it was an accident and he didn't mean it. He was rushing about in a panic getting cotton wool and plasters. The girl knew then she was right about him all along. He was just like Ray Beasley who had hit her when she was four for making too much noise when he was watching football on television.

Then her mum came home. The man was so clever and crafty then. He said there'd been a little accident and maybe it was partly his fault because he'd tried to stop the girl climbing up the shelves but she'd pulled away and fallen. The mother believed him and started fussing over the girl. But the girl could tell her mum was really cross with her, that she thought she was over-acting and being hysterical and difficult and that made the girl even more upset and she screamed, *Why do you always take his side! I hate you!* She ran out and locked herself in her room.

She wants to tell her mum what really happened, but she's so worried that she'll take the man's side again, because her mum's so besotted she won't let herself think that the man would do a thing like that. The girl knows she said lots of horrible things to the

man and made him angry, but he shouldn't
have hit her.

She can't tell her gran either because she's
ill in hospital. At the moment she's too
unhappy to think straight.

Sunday, 8th August

5.45 a.m. I don't feel like me any more. I
didn't sleep much. Mum was banging on the
door for ages, asking me to unlock it so we
could talk about it. Oh yeah? And let **HIM**
come in and start sucking up to me, like Mr
Creepy Nice! No way!

She tried getting in the window too but I
slammed it shut just in time and pulled the
curtains. When I tried talking to her before
she wouldn't listen to me so now I'm trying
not talking to her.

Graeme's litter tray is getting smelly and I
need the loo.

There's a huge bump on my head — it
really hurts. All the blood has soaked through
the plaster and the skin is going purple.

6.20 a.m. Graeme and me have decided to
climb out of the window. We're going down
to the park to get some fresh air.

I don't know what to do.

10.20. THE ACTION MAN HAS GONE! I can't believe it. He's really gone! Mum told him to get out and never to come back. I wish I'd been here to see it.

She says she went frantic when she found my window open and the room empty. She was going to call the police because she knows I'm not the sort of person who goes off without telling her where I am. She was in a real panic and started to search everywhere in case I'd left a note or a clue to where I'd gone. And she found this notebook.

She says her heart nearly stopped when she read the last few days' pages. She couldn't take it all in at first. As it sank in, she started screaming and yelling at the Action Man to get out.

He acted as if he didn't know what she was going on about. So she read it out to him – the bit about him hitting me. She was so angry she started pounding at him with her fists. She threatened him if he wasn't gone in thirty seconds, she'd call the police. So he went.

I was sitting on a bench in the park when all that was happening. Feeling terrible, watching Graeme nibbling the grass, not knowing what to do. Then I heard someone call my name and looked up to see Mum running towards me. I don't know who was crying more, her or me. We sat there for ages. Mum saying sorry, over and over. And both of us grizzling.

Now I want to yell **YIPPEE!** But I can't because Mum looks so miserable and her eyes are all veiny and red. She's all sorry now and wished she had never set eyes on the Action Man. When Nolly comes home from hospital we'll be just like we were before. Another wish has come true. I can't wait for Nolly to come back, then everything will be perfect. We are going to see her this afternoon. We are not going to tell her about the Action Man as we don't want to worry her.

Mum keeps fussing over my cut head and crying and saying sorry she didn't believe me. I've told her it's all right. He's gone now. We've got to forget him.

HE'S GONE! HE'S GONE! It really is true. I've chucked all his tapes and CDs and stuff in a bin bag. Then Graeme and me went shopping and bought some grapes, crisps and

chocs and celebrated in my room. I spelt out
GOOD RIDDANCE! in Cheerios and Graeme
gobbled them up.

Monday, 9th August

Father Coogan was at the hospital when we
visited Nolly. There was a huge bunch of
flowers on Nolly's trolley. I could not believe
it when I saw the card. They were from Ian
Tanner. Mum looks terrible today, all blotchy
and swollen-eyed. She told Nolly she had a
cold but I don't think Nolly believed her. She
asked what I'd done to my head so I said
walked into the shelves.

   For tea I cooked boiled eggs
and drew smiley faces on them
and made some bread-and-
butter soldiers for Mum but
she only ate one soldier. The
waste-paper bin is full of
tissues.

Tuesday, 10th August

I have started sorting my room.
The mess was getting on my nerves. I found
my old All About Me book I made when I was
eight. My favourite joke was:

Knock knock.
Who's there?
Dunup.
Dunup who?

Mum is real mopy so I told her the joke. She only pretended to smile. Gave her Graeme to stroke.

9.50 p.m. Mum's friend Carol came round earlier with some wine. She says Mum is truly heartbroken about the A. Man as she really trusted him. She said, *Your mum blames herself, you know. About what he did to you – hitting you like that.*

Carol thinks people like that ought to be reported. I said, *I just want to forget him, thanks.*

They've been shut in the sitting room for hours. I keep hearing howling noises. I was so worried I knocked on the door. Carol says Mum is just letting out all the anger from her system. Then Mum saw me and started slobbering over me and calling me her little darling baby **Finchikins**. I think she's a bit tipsy. I shall never drink like that.

✩   ✩   ✩

Wednesday, 11th August

The wine only made Mum worse. I had to drag her out of bed this morning. I told her she'd better not be thinking of going into the cupboard under the stairs again because the Action Man isn't worth all that grief — it's not like the tragedy of Dad. That set her off again. All I can get her to eat is Rice Krispies. I lent her some of my aromatherapy invigorating bubble bath that I got for my birthday. That made her weepy too.

Thursday, 12th August

I've had a big shock. Some things Mum's been telling me. They're going round and round in my head. When I woke up Mum was sitting at the end of my bed in her nightie, just looking at me. Her eyes all puffy. I think she'd been there a while. I asked her if she was OK.

She shook her head and kept crying, *Finch, oh Finch,* over and over.

I got out of bed and put my arms round her. *Mum, it's going to be all right. Honest,* I said.

She started sobbing. Really **sobbing**. Shaking with sobs. *It's not all right, Finch! It's not all right!*

She went on like that for ages. I was really worried. I didn't know what to do. I wanted Nolly.

I hated my uncle, Mum said suddenly. *Really, really hated him!*

I said, *Look, Mum – I know all that.*

She said, *No, you don't. Not all of it. There's a lot you don't know.*

OK, I said. *Tell me.*

All I've ever wanted is for you to be happy, she said. *You know that, don't you, love? Because – well – sometimes people tells lies. They tell them for all the right reasons, Finch. They tell them because it's easier than the truth. And they think it's for the best.*

I said, *OK.* But I didn't feel *OK.* I got a horrible sick feeling in my stomach. Who was she talking about? Who'd been telling lies?

Then she said, *There are things I've not been honest about, love. And it's time I told you the truth.* She started on about her aunt and uncle again. How miserable she had been living with them. What a big bully her uncle was. How when she was sixteen one of the girls at school invited everyone in their class to her birthday party. How she longed to go but knew her uncle wouldn't let her.

I said, *Mum, what's this got to do with anything?*

She said, *Please Finch – just listen. It's hard enough as it is.*

She went on about how she waited till her aunt and uncle had gone to bed, then sneaked off to the party and what a brilliant party it was. The girl's parents were away. There were loads of people there, some she'd never even met before, dancing and having a great time. For the first time in ages she could forget her uncle and really enjoy herself. She didn't want it to stop. She stayed for a little bit longer, then a little bit more. Next thing, she was waking up on the carpet, surrounded by loads of others snoring away who'd stayed for the night. When she saw it was nearly six o'clock in the morning she was **terrified**. She'd be in big trouble if her uncle found she'd sneaked out. She raced home.

Her uncle was waiting for her. He went for her, calling her horrible names and hitting her. Then he locked her in her room for the rest of the weekend. It wasn't the first time he'd hit her, she said. It happened regularly. Sometimes she didn't even know why. She says that's why she can't ever forgive herself. That she let it happen to me. First with Ray Beasley. And now with Ian Tanner. And she'd trusted Ian. **Really trusted him** – and now she'll never never trust any man again.

After the party things just got worse. Then one day, Mum saw her uncle's jacket hanging on a chair with his wallet sticking out. Without stopping to think, she grabbed it – it was full of ten- and twenty-pound notes. She stuffed them down her jumper, snatched her coat, and ran. She went straight to the station and jumped on the first train. Hours later, she got off at Fletchley. She found a hostel to stay in and they helped find her a job, which was in Nolly's café. She missed all her school exams but she didn't care. She began to feel happy for the first time in ages.

I said, *And that's when you met my dad, Tom Kellogg.*

Mum shook her head. *Not exactly, love. You see, there's no such person as Tom Kellogg. I made him up.*

I couldn't make sense of what she was saying. *Don't be daft!* I said. *Look! We've got his photo.* She said, *The man in the photo isn't your dad, Finch.*

I didn't understand. Who was the man in the photo then? And if he wasn't my dad, who was he? I was really mixed up. Mum said she'd try to explain. So she did. I can't take it in, I really can't. I'm stopping now. I'm too upset and muddled. I'm going to lie down with Graeme and think about all of this. Why didn't Mum tell me all this before? I've been so stupid.

Friday, 13th August

I haven't been able to think about anything else. Writing it down helps me sort it out a bit.

Mum said that after she'd been living in Fletchley for a while she began to feel ill. She started being sick too, so she went to the doctor.

Mum stopped and looked at me. Then she said, *He told me I was expecting a baby, Finch. But I think I knew that already — I was sort of hoping he'd tell me I wasn't. I was so worried I didn't know how I'd manage and...*

I blurted, *It was the party! That was where you got pregnant wasn't it! With me! Because* by then I'd worked out what must have happened. Mum nodded her head. I started shouting at her. *You mean you got drunk! And you went off with some horrible spotty boy!*

It wasn't like that, she kept saying. *And he wasn't horrible. He was so nice to me and made me laugh.* All the time she was crying. *I know it was stupid – that's why I made up that daft story – and I'd be really upset if you ever did anything so silly, Finch.*

No way! I said. And I wanted to know who this boy was. She says his name was Tom and he was tall and had dark hair. And how he must be a pretty fantastic person because he's part of me – and I take after him not her.

Well, that's easy for her to say! But she doesn't know what it feels like, does she! I don't think it's OK at all!

Anyhow, there she was. Sixteen years old, all on her own and expecting a baby. Nolly found her throwing up one day and sort of guessed. Mum told Nolly everything. About her uncle and the party. That's when Nolly offered to help out and said Mum could have her spare room till the baby (me) was born.

What about Tom – my dad? I said. *Didn't he want me?*

Mum never told him. For all sorts of reasons, she says. She thought about it and talked it over with Nolly. In the end she decided not to. Anyway, she didn't even know his full name, where he lived or anything about him. It only seemed to complicate things.

I was still mixed up. Who was the man in the photo if he wasn't my dad? Why lie that he was? Why tell me his name was Tom Kellogg? Why make up stories like that? I just lay on my bed with Graeme, going over it and crying and crying.

Mum says when I was little I started asking questions. Why did Cassie and other kids have dads and I didn't? Where was my dad? What did he look like? Why didn't we have any photos?

She didn't know what to say. I was only three or something. So she invented a story. About him being this good-looking student with a motorbike. How in love they'd been, all their plans — and how he'd died. She just got carried along with it. She says she almost started believing it herself. It was much more exciting and romantic than her real life. She even used to cry when she got to the bit about the scaffolding falling on him.

Then one day, I asked what my dad's name was. It took her by surprise. There was a packet of Kellogg's Corn Flakes on the table. So she said the first thing that came into her head. Tom...Kellogg. Tom Kellogg. All these

years – all those visits to the library – me believing in a fake dad named after a packet of cornflakes.

I wanted to know where she'd got the photo from. She said I gave it her! I came skipping into the kitchen one day with it in my hand. *Look, Mummy!* I said. *It's my daddy! It's my daddy!*

She says I'd been tidying up my toy cupboard and I'd found the photo stuck at the back of a drawer. She says it must have been there when she bought it from Secondhand Land. The strange thing was he did look a bit like the boy Tom at the party. But weirdest of all was the motorbike. Just like the story she'd made up. She says I was so excited and happy with the photo that she went along with it – pretended he was my dad.

She said, *That's all I ever wanted, love. To*

*make you happy. And it looks like I've messed
up.*

So that's the man in the photo and on my
poster. A complete stranger. I feel like
a freak. I have to go back and rethink
everything.

I've torn up all those stupid posters. But
I've kept the photo. It's weird, but I can't
chuck it out. It's like he's part of me. My
make-believe dad. It would be like murder.
I've put him in my Buckaroo box.

I think Mum looks a bit better now she's told
me. I asked her who else knows all this. She
said Nolly and Carol know. Nolly wasn't too
happy about it but went along with it. And
the Action Man knows too. That really threw
me. How come she'd told him and not me?
All those times I went on about my dad! And
those stupid posters stuck all over the place.
To think that all the while the Action Man
knew! I feel like a total idiot.

I didn't understand why Mum had shut
herself in the cupboard all those times when I
was little – if that big love and heartbreak
story about Tom Kellogg wasn't true. She says
it was a whole package of things. She missed

her mum and dad so much and wished they could have known me. She kept remembering her miserable time with her uncle and aunt. Sometimes she began to think her uncle was right about her — that she really was bad.

And even though I was the best thing that happened to her, she was lonely and I wore her out. I wasn't one of those goody-goody babies. I needed hardly any sleep and was always on the go — she couldn't cope. Sometimes she just wanted to shut everything out. If it hadn't been for Nolly she wouldn't have got through it. Nolly was always there for her.

She told me she'd read some other bits of my notebook too. It made her cry. Not just the things about the A. Man, but what I'd written about her and Nolly. She says she realises how lucky she was to have me and Nolly, and what a terrible mum she'd been, making up all those lies. She keeps saying she'll never ever forgive herself for what Ian Tanner did.

I was crying too by then. I'm so mixed up. I'm angry with Mum and sorry for her all at the same time. It makes me weepy to think of her time with her uncle and aunt. She was only my age when her mum died. I couldn't bear it if anything happened to Mum. I think she's been very brave having me on her own – even braver than I thought. And Nolly is the best gran in the world. I hate Mum's horrible uncle. Nolly is a million times better and kinder than him or her aunt.

I went up to Nolly's and told the Virgin Marys they'd better make her well or Nolly was wasting her time on them. I could feel their eyes looking at me. I know why. It's because I've done something very bad. Only Graeme knows about it. I'm just as mean and nasty as Mum's uncle and aunt. I have to tell someone about it, but I'm scared.

Saturday, 14th August

I shared Mum's bed again last night but I couldn't sleep. My head was swirling with all the times I went on about my dad to the A. Man – and all the while he knew none of it was true. Why didn't he say anything? I feel so stupid. And then there's the bad thing I did. It won't go away. It makes me go all cold and sweaty.

We are going to visit Nolly now. The nurses are getting Nolly to walk about now. She was looking at me strangely today, as if she could read my mind. If she could, she'd see a big worry there. When Mum was talking to the nurse Nolly said, *It's a shame about Ian and your mum. I thought he was just right for her.* I said, *What did he tell you then?* She said, *Nothing, lass. I just use my eyes and my noddle.*

Well, I've written a letter. It's the hardest thing I've ever written. I was just going to turn up and say it. But I needed to get the words exactly right. So I'll just give it to him. Anyway, here's what I wrote:

Dear Ian

I am very sorry. I am sorry I called you those things. I am sorry that I wrote that you hit me. Most of all I am sorry that Mum is so unhappy. And it's all my fault. I really really hated you. I expect you knew that.

Mum has told me the truth about my dad. She told me you knew all about it. I keep thinking about all the times I went on to you about my dad. You could have made me look an idiot then, if you'd wanted, but you didn't.

Even when I lost my temper that day you

were moving the shelves and I clobbered you, you didn't fight back. Even when I acted like you'd hit me and wrote it all down in my notebook, you didn't tell Mum I was a liar. You could have, but you didn't. Instead, you took all the blame.

I've been thinking about that a lot and the only reason I can come up with is that you must love my mum a lot. And you didn't want to hurt her by saying bad things about me. I know she loved you lots because she is very sad and we are getting through lots of tissues.

I don't blame you if you hate me but I can't stand seeing Mum so miserable. That's why I'm writing to you. I'm going to tell Mum the truth. That you didn't really hit me. That you tried to stop me climbing up but I kicked you away and it was my fault that I fell and cut my head on the shelf. I'm going to tell her today at five o'clock. Could you come round then? Because I think she's going to be really mad at me. But if you're here, maybe she'll be so pleased she might forget to be mad at me. I really am very very sorry.

Yours sincerely

Finch

4.10. I've put it through his letterbox. I thought he wouldn't want to see me. And maybe I'm chicken. I'm sure he was in — his van was parked outside.

All I can do is wait now. What I've planned is that when I see him coming down the road, I'll make Mum sit down on the settee and tell her she's got to stay there because I've got a big surprise for her. Then I'll give her a copy of the letter so she understands what happened — then I'll dash off to let him in.

Mum could not believe her eyes when she answered the door and Ian was standing there. It wasn't what I'd planned — he turned up too early. Mum answered the door and started screaming at him to get lost and pushing him out. I had to do a nifty bit of explaining and stand between them like a referee.

I'll never forget her face though when I told her the truth. She started blubbing — with relief and happiness I think. She forgot to be mad at me. Until a bit later when it had sunk in properly what I'd done. She didn't want to believe I'd done something like that.

We were both blubbing then.

But then Ian said what matters is that I've put it right. And that it takes a lot more courage to admit you told a lie than to tell one.

You know, it felt so brilliant when I was writing that story and making up stuff up about him hitting me. All my anger and hate flooded out into it. I was thinking, I'd just love Mum to read this. She'd be sorry then.

All the while, Mum was trying to talk to me through the door, begging me to unlock it. I was imagining punishments for her too, like running away – just long enough to get her worried and make her feel really guilty. I was so angry with her. Suddenly, it came to me. Why not disappear for a few hours and accidentally-on-purpose leave my notebook for her to find? Even though it's full of things that are personal, it'd be worth it, wouldn't it? She'd give him the boot all right. I'd get my own back on the A. Man. And Mum would be wishing she'd listened to me.

I left it open at the right page and slid it under my pillow, just sticking out a tiny bit so she'd see it. Then I unlocked my door and climbed out of the window. I knew she'd read

it. Even though it's got DO NOT READ and
KEEP OUT! and stuff scrawled all over it.
She'd be worried and looking for clues,
wouldn't she? It couldn't have worked better.
Except everything's different now. Because
nothing is what I thought.

All I wanted was for him to go away and
for things to be like they were before. But
they can't be, can they?

Sunday, 15th August

Ian is taking us to see Nolly this morning then
we are going to Thorpe Park. I don't really
want to go.

I wish we hadn't bothered with Thorpe Park.
They were both trying too hard to be nice to
me. It just made me feel worse about what I
did. I had to pretend that I was enjoying
myself. You can't just start being chatty and
friendly to someone you've hated and plotted
to get rid of, can you? I didn't feel like
talking or doing anything. My head was going
over and over all that stuff Mum told me.

I wish Cassie was here. She hasn't even sent a
postcard.

Monday, 16th August

Got a Bugs Bunny postcard from Cassie! It says, Have you won the lottery yet? Get on with it! Back on the 19th. I have missed her so much!

Mum went back to work today. Graeme and I went with her. I helped with setting the tables and chatted to some of the oldies. Graeme was very good and they all had a stroke of him. Alf Cobbley said he kept rabbits when he was a lad but they were for eating. He said there's nothing like a good rabbit pie. UGH! Luckily Graeme was on Elsie Nettle's lap so he didn't hear, or I would have had to cover his ears.

humph...

Ian came with us to visit Nolly. She was so pleased to see him but she was giving me some very strange looks. Sometimes I think she really can read my mind. She's getting through lots of mint humbugs because she misses her ciggies. The social worker at the hospital is trying to arrange things so that when Nolly comes home she'll have a carer looking after her while Mum's at work.

I can't wait to have her home again. I want to tell her everything that happened. I don't want any more lies. But I'll wait until she's well enough. I held her hand and told her I couldn't wish for a better gran in the whole world.

Graeme's the only person I can really talk to at the moment. I don't know what to say to Ian. He's taken time off work so he's here a lot. I stay in my room most of the time.

Tuesday, 17th August

Went to the pet shop with Kayleigh to get some rabbit pellets and guess who was there? **Jay!** (and Dan). My tummy went all fluttery when I saw Jay. He's got the most amazing eyelashes. He was getting some dog biscuits, and hay for his guinea pigs. He has eleven guinea pigs, two dogs and a cat. We are going to see them tomorrow!

Wednesday, 18th August

Jay has got a little house with a huge garden. His dad is quite old with grey hair. His mum was out. There were five of the sweetest squeakiest little baby guinea pigs I have **ever** seen. I'm going to ask Mum if I can have one as a buddy for Graeme for his birthday present.

I was telling them all about St Mon's. Jay says he's against private schools because of his socialist principles. I didn't know what he was going on about, so I copied Mr Buckeridge who was always saying, *What do you mean by that exactly?* It makes you sound as if you know what you're talking about and the other person hasn't quite thought it out properly. Jay said, did I want to live in a country where people are treated as equals or not? I told him, equals. He said that equality should mean the best for everyone, not just those who can afford it. So I said that's why it was against my socialist principles too. He is so clever. I don't think I want to go to St Mon's any more. But I might change my mind if we win the lottery.

This is one of Jay's hairs.
I pinched it off his T-shirt.

Nolly might be able to come home in a week or so!

Thursday, 19th August

We've got Mum and Nolly's rooms swapped over. We are going to decorate Nolly's for her as a surprise. I chose the paint – her favourite colour, peach.

Keep ringing Cassie to see if she's back from her hols. But it's just the answerphone.

Ian just gave me a present. It was a funny-shaped looking parcel. I could feel Mum's and Ian's eyes on me as I unwrapped it, like they weren't sure whether I'd be pleased or not. It was a new leg for my bed. Ian had made it. Not just any old boring leg. But like a pile of books, only made of wood. **It's absolutely brilliant!** But it made me feel bad about how nasty I'd been. All I could do was mumble something like, *Yeah, thanks – it's really nice,* and rushed off to my room. I'm going to paint the books different colours and invent titles for them.

I've planned Graeme's **birthday** party for next Thursday. It isn't going to be a surprise because I accidentally left my drawing of his birthday cake design on my desk and I found him looking at it with a big smile on his face. He's inviting Cassie, Smiffy, Kayleigh, Dan and Jay. I'm going to make a grape and Cheerio cheesecake birthday cake with four carrot candles. Kayleigh, Dan and Jay are going to help make a treasure hunt for him with all sorts of goodies in secret places.

Kayleigh says one of the bed-leg books could be called **Round the World by Bike**, by Major Bumsore. What a corny old joke.

Friday, 20th August

9.15. Cassie just phoned! They got back late last night. She's coming round!

Cassie and I didn't stop nattering. We had so much to tell each other. She brought a little **tartan** waistcoat for Graeme! (It's a doggy one really.) She gave me a Pocahontas nightshirt and a box of fortune cookies. They're like wafery biscuits that have little messages inside them. We only ate two because I want to save them.
Mine said, The present is called the present because it is a gift.

Cassie's said, Make new friends but keep the old. One's like silver, the other's gold.

Which we thought was quite **spooky.**

She's dead jealous of my bookpile bed-leg. She wants me to call one of them, **Too Much Lemonade**, by I.P. Freely.

We've decided that we are not going to let St Monica's split us up. She's sort of getting used to the idea now.

I'm telling her

THE TRUE AND **AMAZING** STORY OF WHAT HAPPENED WHILE CASSIE WAS AWAY. I'm doing it in instalments and acting out the parts. It's a bit like *Eastenders*. We're up to Nolly being rushed into hospital. Cassie's been acting out

HOW MY PAIN OF A BROTHER **RUINED** MY HOLIDAY.

Cassie came with us to the hospital and gave Nolly a box of fortune cookies. Nolly opened one which said, *Never argue with a charging rhinoceros.*

We're going to make a **WELCOME HOME, NOLLY** banner tomorrow.

Saturday, 21st August

The banner is excellent. Cassie painted all the letters like tartan. We've decorated it with Scottish thistles and some rabbits.

There are only two pages left in this book now. I bought a new notebook today for Volume 2. It's blue with clouds on it. Out of seventeen wishes **six** have definitely come true.

Wish 1: Nolly has stopped smoking.

Wish 7: My chest is growing.

Wish 8: Shane Ripley will not be in the same class as me.

Wish 14: I've found out about my dad. And he probably hasn't died.

Wish 16: I am going to sit next to someone really nice. He is dreamy!

And Nolly is getting better.

I've just put Graeme's birthday cake in the oven. Ian was doing the washing-up and Mum was upstairs.

I said to Ian, *I bet you thought I was a*

real pain, didn't you?

He grinned and said, *Yeah.*

I asked him if he hated me when I made all that stuff up about him hitting me. He swivelled his eyes and said, *No. But you scared the* **hell** *out of me!*

He said I was a bit like that charging rhinoceros in the fortune cookie. Mum was too – after she'd read my notebook. He decided it was better not to argue – just get out of the way and wait. He says he wouldn't have given up on us though.

He said, *Do you still hate me?*

I shook my head.

He said, *Well, that's a start isn't it?*

Graeme says he hopes he can have a bit of peace and quiet now. It's been very stressful for him these past few weeks with all the shouting and crying. He's really looking forward to his party and meeting Jay because he's heard a lot about him.

I don't know if it's like Nolly says, that Ian is just right for Mum. I do know they are dead soppy about each other. But they need a little bit longer to get to know each other. I've had years to get used to Mum's untidy ways. It might drive him up the wall. I'm not having him just move in though. If they're really, **really** serious they'll have to do it properly and get married. Graeme says he's always wanted to be a pageboy and he could wear his tartan waistcoat.

This evening we had a Chinese takeaway and watched a video. Ian sat in the middle of the settee with his arm round Mum. I sat at the other end with Graeme. Then after a bit, Ian put his arm round me. We didn't mind. It was OK.

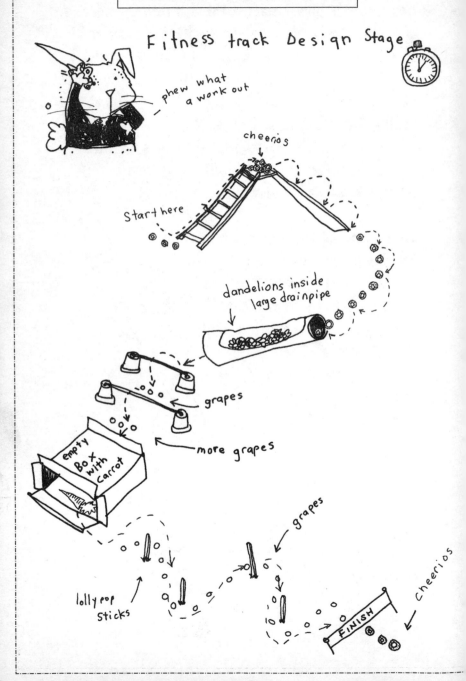

Graeme's Sniff 'n' Dig Course
(Cross section)

carrots   celery   grapes   cheerios   apples

ORCHARD BOOKS
96 Leonard Street, London EC2A 4XD
Orchard Books Australia
Unit 31/56 O'Riordan Street, Alexandria, NSW 2015
First published in Great Britain in 2000
First paperback edition 2001
Text © Pat Moon 2000
Illustrations © Sarah Nayler 2000
The rights of Pat Moon to be identified as the
author and Sarah Nayler as the illustrator of this work
have been asserted by them in accordance with the
Copyright, Designs and Patents Act, 1988.
A CIP catalogue record for this book is available
from the British Library.
ISBN 1 84121 433 7 (hbk)
ISBN 1 84121 435 3 (pbk)
1 3 5 7 9 10 8 6 4 2 (hbk)
3 5 7 9 10 8 6 4 (pbk)
Printed in Great Britain

If you've enjoyed reading
Finch's Top Secrets
as revealed only to Pat Moon,

you may also enjoy these books
by Pat Moon:

Orchard Crunchies

The Jungle Bunch series
Just You Wait, Turtle!
Make it Snappy, Elephant
Ready, Steady, Go, Cheetah!
What's Up, Chimp?

Orchard Black Apples

The Spying Game
*Shortlisted for the Guardian Children's Fiction Award
and the Writers' Guild Award*

Double Image
Shortlisted for the Smarties Book Prize

Nathan's Switch

The Ghost of Sadie Kimber

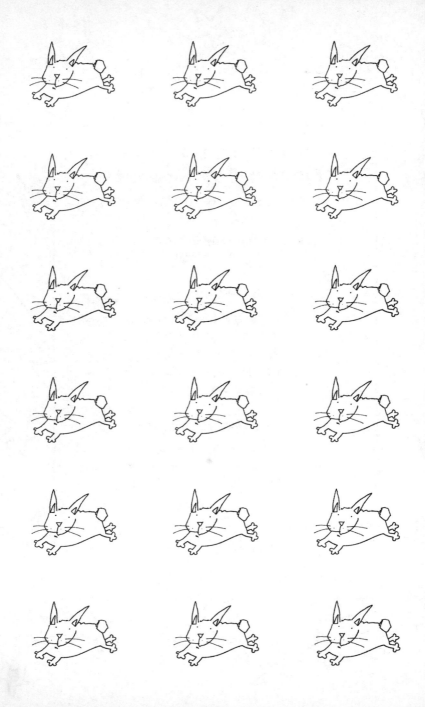